"Ever since you arrived here—"

Danilo stopped abrupt... e
the words past
that quivered w
that stillness be
overpoweringly
presence, his ra
awareness had ju

Tess's pulse leaped as she struggled to drag her eyes from the muscle that was clenching and unclenching in his cheek.

His voice was so deep, it was barely more than a whisper. His expression made every cell in her body want to run away, but for some reason by the time the message reached her brain, it said something different. Her eyes never left his face as she took a step toward him. His hands closed over her upper arms and he impatiently dragged her into him until they were close enough for her to feel the heat of his body, feel the tension in his muscles, inhale the scent of his skin.

It was an unimaginable situation and yet she *had* imagined it. The knowledge came with a rush of head-spinning excitement. Somewhere in the back of her mind, there lingered a small corner, a fragment of sanity that was telling her this was a bad idea, but she determinedly ignored it.

"Say my name."

She swallowed the emotions swirling inside her, making her throat close.

"I want to hear you say it."

Kim Lawrence lives on a farm in Anglesey with her university-lecturer husband, assorted pets who arrived as strays and never left, and sometimes one or both of her boomerang sons. When she's not writing, she loves to be outdoors gardening or walking on one of the beaches for which the island is famous—along with being the place where Prince William and Catherine made their first home!

Books by Kim Lawrence

Harlequin Presents

Visit the Author Profile page at Harlequin.com for more titles.

Kim Lawrence

SURRENDERING TO THE ITALIAN'S COMMAND

ISBN-13: 978-0-373-13955-2

Surrendering to the Italian's Command

First North American Publication 2016

Copyright © 2016 by Kim Lawrence

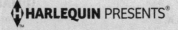

HARLEQUIN PRESENTS®

Printed in U.S.A.

Recycling programs
for this product may
not exist in your area.

ISBN-13: 978-0-373-13955-2

Surrendering to the Italian's Command

First North American Publication 2016

Copyright © 2016 by Kim Lawrence

Printed in U.S.A.

www.Harlequin.com

SURRENDERING TO THE ITALIAN'S COMMAND

For Aunty Pat, a gutsy lady.

CHAPTER ONE

TESS LEANED HER hot forehead against the fridge and struggled to inject a smile into her hoarse voice. 'I'm fine,' she lied. 'I feel a hundred times better.'

'You're a terrible liar,' Fiona retorted.

Tess straightened up and lifted a hand to her throbbing head, responding to the affection in her friend's voice with a weak smile. 'No, I'm a very good liar.'

Only yesterday she had sounded sincere when she'd told her mum's PA that she was *really* sorry she couldn't attend the community centre official opening where her mum was cutting the ribbon. Flu had its plus points—though in this case she wasn't lying, she really *was* feeling better; even so a hundred times better than utterly wretched was still pretty awful.

'I would have dropped in on my way home

but I had to work late. You're not the only one with this flu—half the office is off sick. It's a nightmare. But I'll definitely stop by in the morning after I drop off Sally and the girls at the station. Is there anything you need?'

'You really don't need—'

'I'll be there.'

Tess applied a tissue to her red nose. She was too tired to argue.

'Well, don't blame me if you catch this thing,' she grumbled.

'I never get flu.'

'I think they call that tempting fate,' Tess muttered as she rested from the two steps she had taken, leaning heavily against the work-top counter. It was crazy but her knees were still shaking from the effort of walking from the bedroom to the kitchen.

Fiona cut across her. 'In the meantime make sure you get plenty of fluids—' Tess heard the sliver of sharp anxiety that slid into her friend's tone as she added, 'You did change all the locks?'

'I did everything the police suggested.'

Which amounted to becoming a prisoner in her own flat. She glanced over at the extra bolts that had been fitted to her front door when she'd had her locks changed.

'They should have arrested the disgusting sicko.'

'They raised the possibility of a restraining order—'

The admission drew a gasp from Fiona. 'Then why…?' Followed by an understanding groan. 'Oh, of course, *your mum*…?'

Tess said nothing; she didn't need to. Fiona was one of the only people who understood. She'd been there when, at ten, Tess had become the poster girl for her mum's crusade against school bullying. And Fiona had been there again when her mum had used a tearful image of her at her dad's funeral as part of her campaign to win a local council election.

'She *means* well,' Tess said, unable to resist the knee-jerk reaction to defend her parent. It was true that Beth Tracey—she had reverted to her maiden name after she was widowed—did have the best of intentions, and though she had a genius for self-promotion it was never herself she promoted, but her good causes.

'The rumour is that she's going to put herself forward as an independent candidate for mayor?'

'I heard that rumour too.' Lucky for her, Tess reflected grimly, that her ambitious parent had finally accepted the fact her only daughter was not a political asset, though that didn't stop her trying.

'Even if I had gone down that route there is no guarantee the court would have granted it. He comes across as very...well...harmless. And I had no *proof* he'd even been in the flat. After all, he didn't actually *t...take* anything.' Tess hated the quiver in her voice—she'd sworn not to be a victim.

'What he did was way worse, Tess. That creep invaded your home.'

Tess was glad her friend couldn't see her as her knees sagged and she slid down to the floor. The incident had been the turning point, the moment Tess had realised that ignoring the man, even feeling sorry for him, was not an option. He was dangerous!

Even a month after the event the memory still had the power to send a wave of nausea through her, powerful, but nothing like the sick disgust, the profound sense of violation she had experienced that evening. The rose petals on the bed and the champagne and glasses displayed on the bedside table had been terrifying enough, but it had been the open underwear drawer that had made her rush to the bathroom to throw up.

It was as if her stalker had *wanted* her to know, and yet he had taken great care not to leave any evidence of his identity.

'I know.' Tess cleared her throat and struggled to steady her voice. 'I suppose from their point of view people *leaving* flowers and champagne isn't a major crime.'

'Stalking is these days. Did you tell them about the emails?'

'There was nothing threatening. The police were sympathetic.' Tess had been prepared not to be believed but the professionals had found it easier than she had to accept that the deep and meaningful relationship Ben Morgan believed he shared with Tess consisted only of the odd good morning they had exchanged at the bus stop.

'Well, sympathy is going to be really useful when he stabs you in your sleep one dark night!'

Alerted by Tess's audible gasp, Fiona stopped and hastily backtracked. 'Not that he would, of course. The man's a wimp, a total loser! Me and my big mouth. Are you all right, Tess?'

Teeth clenched, Tess stubbornly fought her way back from the place where Fiona's angry remark had sent her, ignoring the icy fist in her stomach. Her chin lifted. To feel fear meant the crazy had won.

'Nothing two aspirin and a cup of tea won't cure,' she said, struggling wearily to her feet.

'*Turn that thing down, you lot, or I'll switch off the cartoons...* Sorry about that,' Fiona continued, raising her voice above the din that Tess could now hear in the background. 'My dear sister is taking a bath and the twins are running rings around me. Under-fives and a white carpet are not a good combination... *who knew*?'

'You go and save your carpet, Fi.'

'Are you *sure* you're all right? You *sound* awful.'

Tess managed a hoarse chuckle. 'I look even worse.' She pushed a strand of lank hair from her face and turned her back on her distorted reflection in the polished surface of the kettle. A glance in the mirror, when she'd dragged herself out of bed earlier, had already revealed her red nose, dark circled eyes and ghostly pallor. 'But I'm fine.'

A snort of exasperation echoed down the line.

'All right,' she admitted. 'I feel terrible but I'm going to make myself a cuppa and go back to bed.'

'Good plan. I'll see you tomorrow.'

Putting on the kettle, Tess opened the fridge and pulled out an open carton of milk. Her congested nose meant it wasn't until it landed in a congealed gloopy mess in the bottom of her mug that she realised it had soured.

Deprived of it, suddenly all Tess could think about was a cup of tea. The corner shop was less than two hundred yards from her front door…if she took the shortcut through the alley.

Tess, still in her pyjamas, left the flat huddled in the duffel coat that Fiona's boyfriend had left behind the last time he and Fi had come to supper. He was a slight man but the coat still swamped Tess's petite frame.

Slow and steady, she counselled her shaking knees. *Like I have a choice!* She had made it halfway down the alley when she heard the helpful policewoman's soothing voice in her head.

'Look, don't get paranoid. You've done right to remove your online presence—a pain, I know, but the anonymity makes people like this guy feel brave. As for the rest, just take a few common-sense precautions—if you're out stay with friends, and if you're alone keep to public places where there are plenty of people

and the lighting is good. Very often guys like this fasten onto someone else.'

Tess's heart gave an extra-hard thud as she stopped dead, suddenly very conscious of the oppressive darkness that seemed to press in on her.

She had put herself in exactly the sort of situation the police had suggested she avoid.

Teetering feverishly on the brink of panic, she took a couple of deep breaths that made her cough, not calm. The hacking sound echoed off the high walls on either side as she resisted the messages from her feverish brain that made her want to turn around and run. That was a bad idea on two counts: she wasn't capable of running and she was actually closer now to the other side—the main street, where there were lights and people and safety.

'You'll be fine…fine, totally fine, you are not a victim…not a victim…' Her mantra stalled as the figure appeared at the other end of the alley. He barely paused before he began to walk towards her.

Tess opened her mouth to scream and nothing came out. She was living a nightmare, the horribly familiar recurrent one where she was paralyzed. She couldn't breathe. As if some-

thing malevolent were sitting on her chest—
someone malevolent.

'Relax, I'm here to look after you, dar-
ling—'

It was not a scream but it was a noise. Desperately she tried again to raise the alarm…

'Without knowing the details of your sister's
case I can't be sure, but from what you tell me
I doubt very much if she would be a suitable
candidate for the treatment.'

Don't kill the messenger!

Danilo let his eyelids lower to hide his expression before letting the tense breath escape
his lungs in a carefully managed exhalation.

'But if you would like me to see her…?'

Danilo's lashes lifted.

The man sitting opposite saw the question
in the dark depths. 'Obviously you'll want to
discuss it with her?'

'Who?'

'Your sister. I understand that she had already had several unsuccessful treatments?'

From somewhere the memory of the angry
words of the kid he had warned off his sister
the previous month came back to him. *'You
don't want to see me here again, but what
about what Nat wants? She wants to see me,*

and I want to see her. I love her. When are you going to let her live her own life?'

'She wants to walk.'

The man's understanding expression aggravated Danilo, who got to his feet and tipped his head in acknowledgement. 'I will be in touch.'

Her own life.

A life. That was what he wanted for his sister. It was to that end he had taken her to every top spinal expert, he had made himself familiar with every new piece of research. He would not give up, but he would ask her and she would agree with him.

She always did.

Frowning at his annoying inner voice, he waved away the driver who had got out of the limo to open the door.

'I'll walk.'

As he strode, hands dug in his pockets, along the pavement shining from the recent shower, he was lost in his own thoughts so he barely registered the sting of unseasonal hail that began to fall again, quickly covering his hair in icy, white fragments that clung to the dark strands. It was a typical British summer.

There were moments in life where a man was forced to face up to his failings, his weaknesses. He'd been in London the night that he'd faced his, the night of the accident that had robbed his parents of their lives and left his teenage sister in a wheelchair.

He should have been there, he should have been at the wheel of the car, and if he had things might have been different. He'd never know because he'd had a better offer, a night with a beautiful blonde in London. The excuse had come so easily.

Self-disgust churned in Danilo's belly as he relived the moment when the police had finally tracked him down to the hotel room. By that point the city sky had been streaked with morning light and his little sister had been in a hospital bed in Rome fighting for her life for over seven hours. And she had been *alone* because their parents had been lying on a mortuary slab.

He'd put a night of casual sex ahead of duty to his family.

If he'd not been such a selfish bastard… well, who knew? Things *might* have turned out differently. Would his more youthful reflexes have made all the difference? He'd never know; that was his punishment. Compared to Nat, though, he'd got off pretty lightly and she'd done nothing to be punished for, but one thing he did know was that while he had breath in his body he would not stop searching for a cure for his sister.

It was the right thing to do, the *only* thing to do, he had no doubts. And yet…? His frowning contemplation of the wet pavement deepened as he trudged along it with the surgeon's words—*discuss it with her*—floating around in his head. He kept picturing Nat's face the *last* time her hopes had been raised by the promise of a miracle cure and then dashed. She'd looked so bleak.

He shook his head, refusing to acknowledge the doubts in his head. His little sister was the strongest person he knew and he had to stay strong for her, stay positive, and one day she would walk.

He was so deep in his own thoughts that he'd walked past the alley before he registered the sound: a woman's cry, filled with fear. His response was hard wired—there was no question of walking on and pretending he'd not heard. A few seconds later he was at the entrance to the cobbled alleyway; the overhead street light illuminated the scene and seconds told him all he needed to know.

The guy had hold of the woman and she was trying to escape.

Danilo struggled to hold back the red mist that threatened. Bullies were a species that always challenged the objectivity he prided himself on. He could spot one at fifty paces, and like muscle memory the sight of a bully in action always awoke the fifteen-year-old in him, the one who had yet to enjoy a spectacular growth spurt that had seen him grow twelve inches in as many months and the musculature that went with it putting him safely beyond the attention of those creeps in life who looked for victims who were seen as weaker or different.

The man didn't see him coming so he put up no resistance when Danilo took hold of his collar and physically dragged him away from the young woman. One glimpse of her pale face, too pale to be pretty—the cheekbones too sharp, the eyes too big, the mouth…actually the mouth was pretty good—cranked up his chivalrous levels several more notches.

She reminded him of Nat, not that there was any physical similarity. Nat was beautiful, not plain, and his sister was tall, not tiny. Still, he'd not been there for Nat when she'd needed him, but he was here now.

'What the hell…?'

The guy let out a frustrated bellow, flailing wildly, his arms windmilling as he was set down on his feet yards away from the cowering figure of the woman. Apart from her, he didn't look so big—and obviously he didn't feel it either, when he turned and saw Danilo standing between him and his victim.

The aggression in the man's face diminished significantly but the wariness in his eyes was mingled with calculation as he held out his hands and smiled.

'This is a misunderstanding…' He spoke while moving in a direction that would give him access to the woman now hidden from his view behind Danilo.

Danilo negated his ploy by shadowing the move before allowing his glance to linger on the scratch that was seeping blood on the guy's cheek. *Good for her,* he thought approvingly.

'I don't think so. Do you want me to call the police?' he asked the woman without taking his eyes off the other man.

'I just want to go home.'

The hoarse little whisper had a heartfelt sincerity that didn't help Danilo's struggle to resist the impulse to shake the guy until his teeth rattled. Then she sniffed and he almost lost it. Instead he moved to her side.

'Or a hospital?'

'She's fine. *Police...?*' The falseness in the laugh grated on Danilo. 'You've got it all wrong, mate. This was just a misunderstanding. You know how it is. Something and nothing—*sweetheart.*'

In a heartbeat Tess tipped from relief to outright panic. What if this man believed him? What if he left her alone with bonkers Ben?

'I am not your mate.'

It wasn't until her rescuer spoke in a voice that held a twenty-below chill that Tess realised she had grabbed his arm in a death grip. His words made her feel better, but just to be sure she didn't let go; instead she tightened her grip and moved in closer.

'And to answer your question, no, I do not *know how it is* to force myself on a woman.'

'She's mine...'

Ben's voice made Tess's skin crawl. She shook her head in mute rejection. The denial locked in her throat, all she could do was squeeze her eyes closed to avoid the stare of Ben's cold, creepy eyes, but not before it had loosened the lid on the box in her head marked *Don't deal—lose, bury, forget!*

The deeply buried memory that escaped was so clear that for one disorientating moment Tess was sixteen again, cornered by the man her mum was dating. Watching helplessly as he locked the door, his smile and his soft, oily voice making her skin crawl and her insides chill as he told her they could *have some fun*. Tess knew she was lucky she never found out what his idea of fun entailed because it turned out that sleazy creeps did not find it *fun* to have their victim throw up all over their expensive new shoes!

'You know, it's been a long day,' the man beside her drawled.

She clung to the sound of his voice, focusing on the faint attractive accent, letting it drag her free of the memories that even now made her feel unclean, but most of all angry because she had felt weak and helpless. 'And I am not interested in a debate. However, we could move this discussion to the nearest police station?'

There was a silence followed by footsteps. Tess focused on the clean male scent of the man beside her and let it wash away the memory of the sour scent—a combination of sweat and cheap fragrance—that had emanated from her stalker.

The sound of footsteps had faded before her rescuer spoke again. 'He's gone. You can open your eyes.'

Italian… Tess speculated as she tilted her head to look up at the tall stranger. He'd have looked beautiful to her if he'd had a bad case of acne, but he didn't. He was actually incredibly good-looking.

'I could kiss you!' Relief made her more painfully honest than normal, and saying what she was thinking always had been one of her faults. 'But don't worry, I won't. I have the flu.' She let go of his arm and patted the fabric and let out a long fluttering sigh. 'I'm awfully glad he didn't hit you.'

His crack of laughter made her smile too, and as their eyes brushed she realised that he wasn't just good-looking, he was *amazing*!

He had the olive skin tone that went with jet-black hair, an angular face, dramatic chiselled cheekbones, high forehead, his face bisected by a straight nose, yet the austerity of his strong features was offset by an incredibly sensuous mouth.

His smile was pretty incredible too. It made her feel dizzy. But then he wasn't smiling, he was frowning and she was still feeling dizzy; his dark features were swimming in and out of focus in a weird way.

'It's none of my business…'

So why are you making it your business?
asked the exasperated voice in Danilo's head.

Appreciating the meaning of the phrase
weak with relief for the first time, Tess turned
her head too quickly and felt the world spin.

'But don't you think maybe you should be
a little more careful in your choice of boyfriends?' he observed, tempering both his advice and his disapproval. He might feel he was
speaking on behalf of a brother she might have
somewhere, but he wasn't and thank good-
ness for that. One little sister was enough...
Two...? He hadn't been able to keep the one
he had safe.

At least this woman didn't laugh at him the
way Nat had or doubt his qualifications when
it came to relationship advice. What Natalia
didn't understand was that actually he was
perfectly qualified, because for a long time
he'd *been* the man that brothers warned their
sisters not to date.

This woman just looked at him blankly,
eyes wide, as though he were speaking a foreign language. He allowed himself the luxury
of cursing softly in his native tongue, relieved
when he saw comprehension spread across her
face.

'No, he is...never...not...'

Through the rushing sound in her ears Tess could hear her own voice, then there was just the rushing.

Guilt and alarm grabbed at Danilo and he swore again, low and fluently under this breath, as he placed a steadying hand across her shoulders. She sagged like a rag doll and he wrapped his other arm around her middle. It was then he realised several things: she was shaking and, despite her petite appearance underneath the massive coat, she had curves. Only one fact was relevant.

'You're not going to faint.'

He said it in a way that at any other time would have made her laugh. Macho men who thought just saying something made it so always made her laugh. They generally didn't know why she was laughing—alpha males so often had no sense of humour.

She didn't laugh now though. Instead she leaned against the hand that was now pressed between her shoulder blades and hoped like hell he was right.

'I'll be fine.' The world was swimming back into focus and, yes, he was still as impossibly good-looking.

It didn't seem a very realistic statement, considering the unhealthy sheen of perspiration on her pale skin, but he approved of positive thinking, especially when the option was having an unconscious female on his hands.

'Breathe deeply, in and out…no, not *too* deeply.' He steadied her violent sway and left his arm around her waist while he pulled out his phone. He wondered if his plan to fly directly back to Rome was still realistic. 'That's better…'

She'd thought his eyes were brown, and they were incredibly dark, but now as he captured and held her gaze she realised they were midnight blue, like the night sky, and flecked with tiny points of silver that glittered like stars. From nowhere the phrase *soul stripping* came into her head, though actually clinical was more accurate.

She moistened her dry, cracked lips with her tongue and nodded. 'I'm fine now.'

She looked a million miles from fine. 'My car is coming. Where do you live?'

Tess, her heart still pounding though now with relief and not terror, heard herself recite her address like some obedient lost child. 'I don't need a lift. It's just around the corner.' *What else was around the corner?* Bonkers Ben? She shuddered. The mocking nickname no longer worked in making him seem harmless and absurd. He'd been waiting for her... watching? Was he still watching?

The realisation he could extract himself from this little drama sooner rather than later sent a surge of relief through Danilo and for a split second he was sorely tempted to accept the rejection at face value.

Then she looked over her shoulder, the movement fear-filled and furtive—*hell!*

'It's on my way.'

'It is?' She suspected it was a lie but wasn't about to call him on it. The thought of meeting up with her stalker sent a shudder through her.

Concern roughened the edges of his voice as he said softly, 'You're safe now.'

His voice pulled her back from the brink of panic; the unexpected gentleness in it made her want to cry.

'Please don't be nice,' she begged. 'I'll cry. I know I'm being...' *Pathetic.* 'I'm not normally so—' Tess brought her teeth down on her wobbling lower lip and blinked back weak tears. 'He... Ben... He isn't my boyfriend. He just thinks he is.'

Danilo dismissed her explanation with a shrug of his broad shoulders. 'Not my business.' And he had no desire to make it his business, he reminded himself, turning his head as his sister's features superimposed themselves over the pale, pinched face of this young woman, producing a familiar knife thrust of guilt that he didn't try to evade.

'I have a sister not that much younger than you.' The woman was a little older than he had first assumed. 'And I hope if she ever needed—' His sister *had* needed and he hadn't been there.

The woman took a deep breath and Danilo's habitual objectivity slipped as he watched her attempt to regain control. The effort to straighten her slender shoulders sent a jerky convulsive ripple through her entire body; the air left her lungs in a long gusty sigh, but not the tension.

Heavy lids shadowing his stare, Danilo was torn between reluctant admiration and irritation, his irritation reserved for the protective instincts he felt shift and tighten in his chest as a solitary tear escaped the swimming eyes lifted to his. Things got tighter as he watched it slide slowly down her cheek. He had never seen eyes quite that shade of golden amber before.

Her eyes, almond-shaped and framed by thick, spiky black lashes, lifted her face from plain. They were extraordinary. Still, she was *not* his responsibility.

'Well, thank you. I'd be grateful if it's not out of your way, but I'll be fine now—really.'

The delivery started firm and slowly faded, ending on a definite wobble. She looked at him with eyes that made him think of the runt of the litter of golden retrievers his father's favourite dog had produced.

Danilo, promised first choice of the puppies, had, against all advice, chosen the sickly-looking one who everyone had warned would not survive. But that little animal had gnawed its way into his heart with those eyes.

The dog had survived and was still rewarding his decision with unconditional love, though her coat was less glossy than it had been before she'd got old and stiff.

'But if perhaps you could walk with me, if you're heading that way?' Tess was shaking again, her body seized by inner tremors she had no control over. She didn't shrug off the hand that came to rest gently against her shoulder blades. She was glad of the contact while recognising she was acting like the sort of woman she despised: weak, malleable and in need of male support. And this particular

male had an attitude that normally would have
got under her skin.

*Cut yourself a break, Tess, you've got the flu
and you've had a run-in with your unhinged
stalker.*

CHAPTER TWO

'I'M TESS.' IT SEEMED only good manners to tell the man who had saved her from a situation that could have ended up with her being a crime statistic her name.

'Raphael, Danilo Raphael.'

An angel's name. Appropriate given the circumstances, though her guardian angel had the physical appearance of the fallen variety.

They had reached the end of the alley, where she hesitated. Danilo walked past her and out onto the identical-Victorian-house-lined street. 'Right or left?'

Tess didn't immediately respond because she was doing yet another mental regrade of his position on the gorgeous scale! She pressed a hand to her chest to alleviate the breathless sensation.

There were a number of people who could look pretty good in subdued light but a lot less that could look good spotlighted by the artificially white blanching glare of a street lamp. Her fallen angel could take the unkind illumination, probably because there was not a plane or angle on his crushingly handsome face that didn't deserve to be lit up. It was flawless.

But he was not just a pretty face—the rest of him looked pretty awesome too. This was a man who didn't need good lighting or perfect tailoring to set him apart from his fellow men!

As she paused, mouth slightly ajar, he raised a darkly defined brow questioningly. A slither of liquid heat washed through her, the effects of the fever obviously, as she gave her head a tiny shake and, feeling embarrassed, she stepped out, glancing nervously over her shoulder before tilting her head back to reply to his question.

It struck her for the first time that if she were looking for danger, then in a line-up she would dismiss the mild-looking, bespectacled creep who had been stalking her for the past months. Raphael, on the other hand, was not a man anyone would dismiss. He was the living, breathing photofit image of dark, brooding and dangerous to know.

Not just because he was a hundred feet tall

and hard—he'd lifted Bonkers Ben as though he were a rag doll! Her stomach gave a tiny flip as she recalled the tensile strength in the fingers that had curved around her upper arm. This man had a dangerous vibe.

Mum always had said don't judge a book by its cover, which had always struck Tess as ironic even when she was a kid considering how much trouble her parent went to to present the right image to the public. Today it was all about image. Was this rampantly male stranger the product of some image consultant's efforts or did all that come naturally?

'Right,' she said, gesturing vaguely in that direction. The fact was she was never likely to know anything about this enigmatic man with his intimidatingly perfect profile beyond the fact that he had appeared at the right moment, and for that she would always be grateful. 'It's the fourth house along. The one with the red door.'

'This is it.'

Danilo glanced at the row of names beside buttons on the door frame; either this building was larger than it looked or the homes within were the size of shoeboxes. 'I'll see you to your door.'

Tess had enough fight left in her to challenge his *not open for debate* attitude. 'That's really not necessary.'

As she spoke she realised that the long, low car she had been aware of in the periphery of her vision had stopped. Like the man himself, it looked expensive. She nodded in its direction. 'It looks like your lift is here.'

He turned and raised a hand.

'I'll only be a moment.'

Tess watched as he strode over to the car and spoke for a moment to the driver. She was tempted to slip inside but being caught before she had closed the door on him would have been embarrassing, not to mention ungrateful. And there was the fact it was not exactly hard work to watch him; not only was he supremely elegant, but every move he made suggested a physical power that was riveting.

He returned a moment later and nodded towards the door. 'After you.'

'Fine,' she sighed out as she stepped a little ahead of him into the hallway. 'I'm on the top floor.' The curved staircase and the encaustic tiles underfoot were about the only original features left in the building which had been unsympathetically 'modernised' back in the seventies.

'Where is the lift?'

'We don't have one.' The trick, she told her shaking knees, was to take one step at a time—literally. *This might take some time!*

She had gone up the first three steps, the situation not made easier by the man behind her who was vibrating silent impatience, when she heard a soft growl.

His flight might not be an option now, but at this rate he'd be here half the night and she'd be on her knees by the time she got to the top floor. Sure, the woman was remarkably plucky, but he'd always thought *plucky* was another word for *stubborn*.

It was all a bit of a blur as one moment Tess was holding onto the bannister, and the next she was being casually lifted up into his arms. She grabbed the fabric of his jacket as he strode onwards and upwards.

'Quite unnecessary,' she gasped, sounding a bit like one of those heroines who fainted a lot and got rescued by dashing heroes—she gave a laugh. She was so *not* that girl!

'I was losing the will to live.'

Tess kept her eyes straight ahead, aware of the occasional waft of warm breath on her cheek, trying to retain as much dignity as possible—*a bit late for that!* The hardness of his chest, the warmth, the false intimacy of the situation—all lent another layer of disorientation to what had been a very disorientating experience!

Outside her door he put her back down on her feet.

'You're very kind.'

His jaw clenched. 'I am not kind.'

'Well, I think you are.' She fished in one of the deep pockets for her key. 'So thank you, and goodnight.'

For the first time Danilo noticed there was something quite stubborn about her rounded chin. He found his eyes sliding lower down the column of her neck, the swanlike curve exposed now as she unfastened the top button of her ridiculous coat. She was too pale and too thin but her skin had a flawless, almost translucent quality. He scrutinised her with casual curiosity, wondering what she'd look like if she didn't dress like a reject from a charity shop.

'Not that good a night for you.'

She gave a sigh. It looked as if he wasn't going until she was inside. Flipping her hair, which hung in wet rats' tails down her back, off her face, she made a frustrated sound through clenched teeth. Her hand was shaking so hard she couldn't fit the key in the lock.

'There's a knack,' she panted, her breathing almost as erratic as her heart rate while ironically the man who had just carried her up three flights of stairs was not even breathing hard. He might not be breathing hard but she could feel the impatience rolling off him in waves. It didn't help.

As her frustration built Tess resisted the impulse to kick the door. Instead she rested her forehead on the door and jiggled the key once more.

Her sigh was one of intense relief when it finally opened. She reached for the light switch and stepped inside before turning around. 'Thank you again. I'll be fine now.'

Danilo, his head ducked to avoid the low beams in what had presumably started off as the servants' quarters in the house, nodded, half turned and then lost the fight with his conscience.

He closed his eyes and sighed. He really *wanted* to walk away. He wanted to listen to the voice of common sense that was urging him not to get involved, the same voice reminding him that this was none of his business, that no good, as his English nanny years ago had been fond of darkly warning, would come of it!

But inevitably the tug of guilt was too strong to resist.

'You don't look fine.' That was a massive understatement. Under the strong electric light her face was the colour of paper, the shadows circling her eyes so dark they looked like bruises.

Well, I can't argue with that! Tess's own gaze collided with the critical stare of her dark-eyed rescuer—no man should be allowed eyelashes that long—and stopped. She had just had a close encounter with her own personal stalker, she was struggling to stay upright on knees that felt like cotton wool and she was worried about how she looked… Tess put it down to the temperature she was inevitably running.

'Can I call someone for you?' It was called passing the buck and seemed like a very good idea. 'You shouldn't be alone.'

Alone. The word echoed around in her head in an unpleasant way that made her glance for reassurance at the row of locks on the door. Of course she shouldn't be alone. She *should* and *would* have been enjoying her third day of a fortnight in the sun with Lily, the classroom assistant, and Rose, who taught the other reception class, if it hadn't been for this wretched flu bug.

Her wistful thoughts went to her friends enjoying sun, sea and maybe even a bit of romance and she felt a twist of envy. The only other person she could call on was Fiona, and though she knew her friend would drop everything if she knew what had happened Tess had no intention of spoiling Fiona's last night with her sister and nieces, who lived in Hong Kong. This much-anticipated visit was rare.

There was her mum, of course, and she'd come running. As ambitious as her parent was, she had always put her daughter's welfare ahead of her career, a fact Tess hadn't always appreciated, but if her mum knew what had happened and got the full Bonkers Ben story then by the morning Tess's story, and her name, would have gone viral and appear in every newspaper, while her mum, looking glamorous, caring and just the sort of person you'd *want* to vote into office, would be doing the rounds of the breakfast TV programmes. When she had a cause her mother was relentless and self-promotion came as naturally to her as breathing, neither of which in themselves was a bad thing, but Tess knew from experience what it felt like to be at the centre of one of her mum's campaigns, and maybe she was selfish but she hated the idea of being stigmatised as a victim almost as much as she hated the idea of the attention.

Tess squeezed her eyes shut, but remained aware of the dark, brooding presence. His height was emphasised by the sloping beams. She didn't need her macho guardian angel to tell her she'd have to deal with the Ben situation; she already knew that. But not tonight. If she thought any more her head might explode.

Tess opened her eyes. 'I think—' She blinked. She hadn't invited him and she hadn't been conscious of him moving, but he was standing in her hallway. The presence that earlier had felt comforting now, in the enclosed space, tipped over into disturbing.

'There isn't anyone,' she blurted, then, conscious that might have made her sound as if she had no friends, she added tiredly, 'All I need right now is to sleep off this flu.'

'So what happened back there, you're going to act like it didn't happen?'

His disapproval hit an exposed nerve. 'I'm trying,' she gritted, feeling a flash of irritation with him for hanging around asking questions and making it impossible for her to do just that. Close on the heels of irritation came guilt; he had rescued her.

Danilo's gaze travelled from her face to the

row of locks on the door and his face hardened as he translated what he saw. He felt the hot fury rise in him and fought to damp it down to a low simmer. There were relationships that went sour and then there were people who… His fists clenched as he thought about what in a perfect world would happen to bullies and cowards.

'Your boyfriend from the alley?'

She nodded tiredly. '*Not* boyfriend,' she said without any real hope he'd believe her. His sardonic expression suggested she was correct in this assumption. She opened her mouth then closed it, shaking her head, trying to tell herself that it didn't matter what a total stranger thought.

Teeth gritted, she focused on unfastening the toggles of her man-sized duffel coat, though size was all a matter of perspective, and for that matter so were men, she mused tiredly. While Fiona's boyfriend, Matt, was an average-sized guy, she was lost inside his coat. She couldn't think of any circumstances where she'd be wearing any garment belonging to the man whose eyes she could feel on the back of her neck, but they'd have to send in a rescue team with tracker dogs to recover her if she ever did.

The visual dragged out a laugh between huffs of exhaustion as she struggled with the coat.

The gurgle brought a flash of angry incredulity to his eyes. Was Tess so used to having boyfriends rough her up that she could laugh about it? His jaw tightened. Tales of abusive relationships never failed to outrage Danilo. The men were easy to understand—they were inadequate bullies, and his contempt for them was absolute. But he could never understand why some women always seemed to go back to them, believing that things would change.

It is not your role, Danilo, to lecture this woman on self-respect and personal safety, but the reminder didn't lessen the knot of anger in his chest.

Tess continued to struggle with the coat that felt like a ton weight on her sore shoulders. In fact every inch of her hurt and his scrutiny wasn't helping. The man could communicate more with silences than most people could with a three-page speech, and this time it was disapproval she was getting. No doubt he was just willing her to get a move on so that he could get back to his own important life. Did he think she didn't want that too? She gave a sigh of relief when the last toggle gave and the coat landed on the floor with a thud. She made no attempt to pick it up as she turned back to her rescuer.

'Thought I might have to sleep in it. Look, thank you for what you did.' She stopped when she saw he was still staring at the door.

Danilo could feel the pressure in his head as the anger beating inside his skull reached critical level.

'You should not have to live like this!' He flicked one of the locks with a long finger and spun around to face her, conscious as he did so that he'd just missed his chance to walk away. 'It is outrageous! *Madre di Dio!* How long has this been going on?'

'Please, I've already had this conversation once tonight. Nothing as bad as this has happened before,' she added, feeling the irrational need to defend herself.

'But something has happened before?' He seized on the comment. 'Do you still have feelings for this man?'

The question astonished her. 'I've never had feelings for him. I barely know him.' Or you, she wanted to add, but she didn't because she wanted more for this to be over and for him to go away. Didn't he know that guardian angels appeared at the right moment and then slipped away, silently, without comment, without giving a person a headache—a *worse* headache?

'What are you wearing?'

In the middle of sliding off the scuffed running shoes she had slipped on as she'd left the flat, Tess stopped, a deep flush travelling over her pale skin as her eyes moved from the onesie, chosen for its comfort value and not glamour, to his face.

'Pyjamas!'

'Yes, pyjamas,' she said, beginning to get irritated now. 'Maybe you don't wear them but I do.' She stopped, the colour in her cheeks deepening—*you just suggested he slept naked.*

If only her embarrassment had stopped there but, no, now she'd said it she was thinking it too. Tess was seeing a total stranger naked!

'You deserve better!'

Danilo had no idea where the words came from as he stood there, his embarrassment concealed behind a stony mask—he could assume that his seeming inability to walk away, duty done, conscience salved, was down to that initial nebulous connection he had made between her and Nat. He couldn't save his sister, he had failed Nat, but he could save this woman, who seemed to have serious self-destructive issues.

It was a statement that Tess couldn't take issue with, though she was uncomfortably aware that people rarely got what they deserved.

'He really isn't my boyfriend, though, like you, he *thinks* he is, he even tells people that he is, but in reality he is just a guy who uses the same bus stop as me. There is nothing more between us than small talk.

'At first,' she admitted, 'I just thought he was sweet…then, it was all a bit insidious, really. He'd turn up places I was, outside school, and then there were the emails and the texts. I thought if I ignored him he would get fed up and go away, then last month I had a break-in. There's no proof it was him. He didn't take anything but he left roses and champagne and…well, I took advice and precautions.'

Danilo heard her out in silence, his anger towards the other man growing as she told her story. 'I should have throttled the guy!'

'Well, with any luck I gave him my flu!' The grimly vindictive wish was so out of sync with the wan, pathetic figure standing there that he laughed. The sound drew her attention back to him. 'I hope you don't catch it.'

'You should inform the police.'

'He didn't actually hurt me, or even threaten

to, it's just that I panicked. If I hadn't—if I'd just talked—'

'You were not to blame for what happened.'

'I know that, I'm just saying that I could have handled it better.' Actually what was she saying? She pressed a hand to her aching head. 'I suppose I will contact the police, but not tonight.'

'*Suppose?*'

Tess squeezed her eyes closed. 'If you yell I warn you I will cry and it is not a pretty sight.' Bending forwards as she was convulsed by a loud sneeze, she raised her head and found a box of tissues extended to her. She took a bunch and blew her nose loudly then, looking at him through watery eyes, rasped, 'Thank you.'

'So what are you going to do now?' he asked, tuning out the voice in his head that said, *Not your business*.

With a sigh she turned her back and moved towards the kitchen area that was sectioned off by a breakfast bar. 'I never got my milk for my cup of tea so I'm going to improvise,' she informed him, pushing her hand to the back of the cupboard where a bottle of sherry and the cooking brandy lived.

Standing on the other side the breakfast bar,

circa the nineteen seventies, like the rest of the place, he watched as she took the brandy bottle and glugged some in the bottom of one of the mugs that sat on the draining board. 'Sorry, where are my manners? Would you like some?'

He looked at the label, a flicker of amusement moving across his face. 'Thanks, but I'll pass. Are you sure you should?'

She had enough energy left to silence him with a red-nosed killer look but not enough to get herself to the comfy armchair. She collapsed instead onto the sofa, glass in hand. Then, head pushed back into the cushion, she closed her eyes and took a swallow, choking a little as the raw alcohol burned her sore throat.

'For a woman who is being stalked you are pretty trusting.'

Tess forced her heavy eyelids apart… *Trusting?* The point was she *wasn't*. In fact by some people's more relaxed standards she was paranoid, thanks in no small part to the long-ago incident with her mum's boyfriend. It didn't take therapy to figure out that the episode had left her with some trust issues. Though now was definitely *not* the moment for a forensic analysis of her non-existent sex life.

But maybe, she mused, her eyes drawn almost against her will to the hard angles and planes of the dark lean face of a man who exuded raw sexuality like a force field, it was the moment to wonder why it had not crossed her mind at any point tonight to feel threatened by this total stranger. Down to the fever or plain stupidity?

'Wait, you're not about to tell me you're also some sort of freak who's fallen desperately in love with me?'

He laughed. 'No.'

She lifted a hand to find her ear torn, the blood already caking. So it wasn't just her ear-ring she'd lost but her sense of proportion too—his laugh hurt!

She let the amusement in his voice wash over her, not out of choice but because she had reached the point where stringing two words together was an effort. The dignified high ground was a place Tess aspired to occupy, but she'd never made it there.

On a good day—actually, any day but this one—she would now be informing him that she scrubbed up pretty well, as it happened, and that she had plenty of offers, which would have been childish, but true.

She had moved on a long way from the sixteen-year-old with the bad case of acne, braces and no discernible curves that had inspired the sleaze whom she had so conveniently thrown up over. He'd been less than happy about her obvious rejection of his unwanted advances, enough to issue a disgusted parting shot—*'You should be grateful I'd even look at you!'*

The voluptuous curves had never materialised but two years later her skin had cleared, she had lost her braces and boys her own age had started noticing her. The trouble was their interest rarely lasted long, or, for that matter, was mutual.

Tess had discovered she seemed destined to attract the sort of man who equated her appearance and her small frame with a fragility she did not possess either physically or mentally.

No matter how good-looking a man was, Tess found it a massive turn-off when he treated her as if she were a china doll that might break, and when they discovered she wasn't sweet and yielding, but actually quite tough, they tended to drift away disillusioned—all except Ben, of course.

The man who loved her for who she was turned out to be certifiably insane—maybe, she mused, that was what it took?

She fervently hoped not.

Tess didn't really know who her perfect man was, but she knew he wouldn't patronise her and he would treat her on equal terms. And if he could offer some mind-blowing sex that would definitely be a plus, but so far she had not come close to it!

Of course, while she was telling herself she was waiting for the right man and that she wasn't going to be pressurised into *settling*, it occurred to her that she might be one of those women who were never going to meet the man who pressed all the right buttons. The women who blamed the men because they didn't want to face the possibility it might be them? That they…*she* didn't have it in her? A bubble of rebellion came to the surface of her drifting thoughts: *no, I want passion!*

'I suppose you think that it was something I did?'

'You can't go through life worrying about what other people think. Are you awake?'

'Unfortunately, yes.'

The dry comment made him smile. He could think of few people who could retain a sense of humour after the evening she had had. 'Did you hear what I said?'

'You don't love me—I'm still recovering.'

'Then that's a no. I have a suggestion.'

'Another lock? A remote cottage on the Outer Hebrides? Already thought of it.'

'Your door won't take another lock and it rains too much in the Hebrides.'

When did this Englishwoman become your problem?

Obviously she wasn't his problem, except in the sense she had evoked such a strong protective response in him, which was as difficult to ignore as a kick in the chest.

Try harder!

He responded to the suggestion from his dark side with a thin smile, which morphed into a frown as his dark veiled glance lifted from the tiny defenceless figure on the sofa and slid to the door with its rows of locks. All he had to do was walk through it. He'd done what anyone could expect of him and more.

So *why* was he still here?

Because he knew about the price of selfish actions, he lived with guilt, it was a constant presence in his life and he didn't want any more.

And it wasn't about playing the hero. That would, he reflected, his lips forming a fleeting sardonic smile, have been a serious case of miscasting.

When he thought of heroes he thought of his

little sister. She was the most heroic person he knew. Bleakness drifted to his eyes. Maybe, he speculated, that was why he felt such a strong compulsion now he couldn't save Natalia, but he had the opportunity to save *someone*… His lips twisted in a cynical smile—it helped that it required little or no effort on his part and no sacrifice.

'That stuff is actually quite good.' She leaned back, feeling quite mellow as the glow from the cooking brandy in her stomach began to spread. The floating feeling was pleasant.

'When are you back in college?'

'School,' she corrected sleepily, and yawned as she watched him through the mesh of her lowered eyelashes. At a purely aesthetic level he was well worth looking at. A few sleepy moments later she realised that he was looking at her, not lost in admiration, but because she hadn't answered his question—now, what was the question?

'I teach,' she slurred tiredly. The virus and the events of the last hours were catching up with her big time.

Danilo blinked. 'You're a teacher?'

'No, I'm an *excellent* teacher,' she rebutted with a half-smile, then yawned.

Danilo, still making the mental adjustment,

didn't register her attempt at humour. 'So what do you teach?'

'After I graduated I did some supply teaching, then for a term I was a support classroom worker for a little boy with muscular dystrophy, now I teach reception class.' She gave a self-conscious little grimace, aware that she had given away more information than the casual question required.

'A teacher with experience of...' Encountering the puzzled, expectant gaze lifted to his face, he tipped his head slightly. 'Bear with me... This man tonight, he knows where you live?'

Tess closed her eyes. 'Thanks for that comforting parting shot. I'll sleep better for it.'

'I am not trying to be comforting.'

'Imagine my shock.'

'I am trying to offer a practical solution. The fact is he has broken in here once and I wouldn't put it past him to try a stunt like that again. So, as I see it you have two options. You can go down the legal route or—'

'Live in fear?' she interrupted with a bitter laugh. 'I hate to interrupt this little motivational speech, but—'

'Come to Italy. Your stalker won't find you there.'

She could only assume he was trying to lighten the mood. 'Why not Australia? I've always fancied a bit of surfing.' She opened one eye. 'Don't do comedy, it's not you.'

'My little sister, Natalia, lives at home with me, work takes me away often—'

'You're offering me a job as a childminder?'

'Natalia is almost nineteen.' His dark eyes moved in an assessing sweep over her face. 'How old are you?'

'Twenty-six.'

'There was an accident and my sister is temporarily in a wheelchair. Her life has been on hold, most of her school friends have moved on…away… I think she feels isolated sometimes.' His focus had been so much on pushing forwards with Nat's recovery that it could be argued he had virtually pushed her into the arms of that no-hoper Marco.

It could happen again, and he couldn't be there for her all the time, but if she had someone there her own age, another woman to confide in… 'I think it might help her.'

'I'm sorry.' The picture he painted touched her deeply. 'Your parents…?'

'Were killed in the same accident.'

A powerful wave of empathy swept through Tess, almost painful in its intensity. She squeezed her eyes tighter closed over the hot sting of unshed tears and cleared her throat before responding huskily.

'I'm so sorry.' It seemed lame but what else could she say?

He cut a sideways look at her before tipping his head in acknowledgement.

'But I couldn't.'

'Why not?'

Indignation gave her the strength to lift her heavy eyelids. 'Are you serious? I can't just up and leave—' She stopped and thought, *or could she?*

It would solve the immediate problem, give her a breathing space to decide what to do about Ben and she was missing out on her holiday. She'd always wanted to see Italy.

'The decision is yours,' he said, giving the impression that he'd lost interest in the subject. 'When you have decided…' He pulled a card from his breast pocket and looked around for an empty surface to put it on before handing it directly to Tess.

'This is the number of my assistant in London. She will coordinate things on this end, flights and so forth. She will take up your references. I was thinking that you could travel at the end of the week, either Thursday or Friday, unless your cold doesn't clear up.'

'I have flu,' she countered automatically. 'You want references?'

'Is that a problem?'

'No, it is not a problem.'

'When I leave you will lock the door.' Slinging the edict over his shoulder, he walked through the door.

It was around two in the morning when Tess woke up on the sofa, the business card clutched in her hand. She glanced over to the unlocked door and shivered. Well, she'd slept a little at least, no doubt the result of combining the brandy with the cold and flu meds she'd been liberally popping in an attempt to feel better. She looked at the card again, reading out the name printed on it in bold italics.

Danilo Raphael.

She would consider his offer but only after she had locked the door.

CHAPTER THREE

WHEN SHE TOLD Fiona of her plan the next day her friend was horrified.

'You're mad, crazy. You have no idea who this man is!' She looked at the business card he had handed her. 'Anyone can get one of these printed. For all you know he could be a pervert—'

'Give me some credit, Fi, I'm not an idiot. I looked him up online. He's legitimate.' He was actually a bit of a legend in his own lifetime, but, afraid of being accused of exaggeration, Tess didn't share these details. Instead she picked up her phone, scrolled down on the screen and handed it to Fiona—it was simpler.

Her friend took it without looking and snorted. 'Online I'm *legitimately* a size ten. People make stuff up all the time—' She glanced down and took a deep breath, the expression of awe that spread across her face almost comical. 'Wow! *He* rescued you?'

'I like to think of it more that he happened along at the right moment.' And what would have happened if he hadn't? Tess pushed the question away. Some things it was better not to know and she already had enough problems sleeping.

Fiona couldn't take her eyes off the phone screen. 'He *really* looks like that? This photo's not airbrushed or anything?'

'Well, he looks a bit older.' Harder, would have been more accurate. In the flesh Danilo Raphael possessed a streamlined lean toughness that didn't come across in the photos online, and there had been a lot to compare and contrast, but most were of him looking younger though still dramatically good-looking. The camera really did love those cheekbones, and so, it seemed, did the wide selection of women pictured draped all over him.

'He's a hottie!'

Tess chose to ignore Fiona's comment and folded the last item in her case. She huffed gently as she closed the lid. 'I hate packing and I never take the right thing,' she complained.

'You look good in a bin sack,' her friend consoled. 'If I had your figure…well, never mind that. So,' she said, handing back the phone, 'what does *gorgeous* do when he's not rescuing women?'

'Makes money.'

'He's sounding better all the time.'

'It seems he buys failing companies and makes them work, or at least he used to. He took over the family firm when his parents died a couple of years ago, and they had pretty much a finger in any pie you care to mention...' Tess mentioned a few. 'After their death, though, he dropped off the party circuit—'

'Got married and had a few kids?'

Tess managed to conceal her reaction to the question and shrugged. She had no idea *why* the idea of Danilo Raphael enjoying domestic bliss shocked her so much, but her friend's analysis of the low public profile did work.

'Maybe?' The information she had about the accident online was sketchy. The headlines were lurid and, though there was little detail, she felt safe assuming that this was what had brought about the change in this ex-playboy's lifestyle.

'You do realise what you described is called asset stripping? And asset strippers are not a breed noted for their warmth and human kindness.'

'He said he wasn't kind,' she remembered. Strangely, despite the trauma and her fever she could remember every word he had said and the exact intonation of his husky voice. She caught Fiona looking at her and carefully wiped away whatever expression had been on her face that had made her friend stare. 'But I'm hired to be a companion to his sister, not hold hands with him.' An image floated into her head of his long brown fingers; she pushed it away. 'I doubt if I'll even see him.'

One step through the door and Danilo swung back, the expression on his lean face impatient as he gave a shrug and responded to Franco's question.

'She's petite, maybe even a little mousey, she's probably looking lost…big eyes in a small face.' His mouth quirked as the description brought a disappointed look to his cousin's face. 'What were you expecting, a supermodel?'

His cousin gave a grin. 'It wouldn't have hurt. So what do you want me to do with this mouse?'

'Drop her off at the house. Nat is expecting her.'

'You don't expect me to stay and babysit,

then? I'm meant to be meeting the event organiser later this morning.'

'Your cousin Angelica will look after her and introduce her to Nat.' The furrow between his dark brows deepened. 'More problems with the party?'

'Just a few tweaks. I want it to be perfect.'

'That is the general idea,' Danilo agreed, holding eye contact long enough to see his cousin squirm. The lie was obvious but Danilo, already late for a meeting, let it lie.

'So I can just dump her and run?'

Tess, who had adjusted her step to accommodate the slower pace of her travelling companion, was about the last person from the London flight to clear the customs checkpoint, and as they entered the arrivals lounge together the elderly Italian lady was immediately surrounded.

The size of her laughing family was equalled by the number of kisses being exchanged. The warmth and volume of their greeting was overwhelming, and for a moment Tess shared the warmth and was literally swept along by it, until a young man kissed her and then drew back, blushing with teenage embarrassment as he quickly apologised for his mistake.

'Signora, mi dispiace.'

The old lady, laughing, took Tess's hand and introduced her.

'This is Tess, who held my hand during take-off and landing.'

'It was a mutual thing. I was terrified too.'

'Is there someone here to meet you?' the man who had identified himself as her travelling companion's son asked.

Tess nodded, her eyes sweeping the area, refusing to acknowledge the tiny blip of anticlimax that tightened in her stomach. It wasn't as if she had expected even for one moment to be met personally by Danilo Raphael.

'I think that might be him over there.' She nodded towards the only person remaining, a young man in a designer suit who stood with hands in his pockets scanning the room impatiently and glancing up at the arrivals board at intervals. 'Excuse me, and congratulations on the birth of your first grandchild,' she added with a smile.

'Excuse me?'

The scowl on Franco's face lifted a little as the petite woman with the long glossy hair, wearing a pair of spiky ankle boots and a swingy little skirt that showed off her slender, shapely legs, stopped right in front of him. For a moment it seemed less important that Danilo was going to blame him for the no show of the English mouse.

Franco swallowed, his heart beating a little faster as she smiled. It was a really great smile.

'By any chance are you looking for me?'

'All my life, *cara*.'

The extraordinary amber eyes continued to meet his with a directness he was beginning to find unnerving. One of the feathery dark brows rose. She gave a kind smile and observed, 'Which is not actually so very long, is it?'

Feeling like a schoolboy and not enjoying the novelty value—he might not be able to impress his older cousin but young females were normally putty in his hands—he felt his face colour.

'I'm sorry, but you seemed to be looking for someone, so I thought perhaps you'd been sent to meet me by Mr Raphael?' She blinked away the intrusive image of the Italian's dark, strongly sculptured features and focused on the handsome and far less disturbing face of the young man she was addressing.

'You're the m... Mou...' Franco shook his head and allowed his eyes to drift to the pink pouty lips. 'I think,' he said regretfully, 'there has been some mistake.'

The words echoed the thought that had been fighting to make itself heard in Tess's head ever since she had boarded the flight. Was she making a colossal mistake here? She gave her glossy head the slightest of shakes and straightened her slender shoulders, pushing away the doubt. Mad or not, she'd made her decision and she was going to make the best of it.

'I should have introduced myself. I'm Tess Jones.'

Franco's jaw dropped, before moments later a smile spread across his features. 'And I'm Franco. Danilo said… Sorry, I was expecting someone…not you,' he finished awkwardly. 'Danilo is my cousin.'

'Well, that's a relief.' She arched a curious brow. 'Who were you expecting?'

Franco sidestepped the question. 'I thought you were with your family?' Franco nodded towards the group who were gathered around the elderly lady that the stunning English girl had appeared with.

The curious pucker between her feathery brows smoothed as she accepted the explanation. 'Oh, the Padrones.' She lifted a hand

and waved. 'No, I've never met them before. Carlita and I just bonded over our fear of flying. We got talking and she's quite a character and so proud of her family. Her youngest daughter lives in London—she'd just had her first child.' Tess tucked the woman's address into her bag and waved once more to the family who were moving towards the exit.

'Where exactly did Danilo find you?'

For the first time her candid gaze fell from his.

'Long story but he was very…kind.' Not sold on the accuracy of her description, Tess absently rubbed the frowning indent above the bridge of her small straight nose as one of the jumble of memories that had imprinted strongly surfaced.

For a disorientating moment the weight of a muscled arm draped across her shoulders was so real that she inhaled, anticipating the spicy fragrance with minty overtones she recalled.

She inhaled again, this time to focus, feeling irritated with herself. There was no point coming to Italy to escape if you brought the bad memories with you.

Danilo? Kind? While his cousin was one of life's good guys, he was not what most people would call kind. Franco managed to maintain a bland expression while his imagination went into overdrive.

It was midnight by the time Danilo drove his car past the security cameras mounted on the gates that swung open as he approached and closed behind him as he drove down the familiar mile-long tree-lined driveway that led to Palazzo Florentina, the Tuscan home that had been in the Raphael family for generations now. The home he had returned to after his parents' deaths.

The road split just as the distinctive building with its central golden stone tower, spotlit in the darkness, came into view. He drove along the right-hand fork and through the arch into the well-lit courtyard, built from the same distinctive stone as the main house.

Once, when the place had been the summer home of a royal family who had built the place—there was a *tenuous* family link to the Raphaels—all of these buildings would have been the stable block. Nowadays only one wing housed horses. So far Danilo hadn't been able to bring himself to reduce the number of animals. His mother had been a keen horsewoman and had adored each and every one, so he justified his economically irrational action, or lack of it, by promising himself that he would ride more—when he had the time.

He approached the wing opposite where the horses were housed in luxury, heading for the garages that took up another wing. The rest had been converted into accommodation. The largest staff apartment was occupied by a distant cousin. Since the death of her husband, Angelica had taken on the role of housekeeper, and her apartment was the only one that had its own garden.

He didn't bother raising the automatic doors; instead he parked on the cobbles, glancing up as he got out at the section of the buildings where Franco had an apartment. No lights showed at the windows, but then his young cousin rarely spent a night there if he had a better offer, which he frequently did. He'd probably crawl into work late tomorrow looking like hell!

Danilo's lips quirked as he recognised the irony of his disapproval—or was that envy? He was hardly in a position to judge considering that there had been a time not so long ago when he'd been the guy who partied most nights and the photos still existed to prove it.

Not that he led the life of a monk now—he

knew his limitations—but nowadays his sex life was more…*discreet.* Discreet and disposable. He smiled without humour to himself, liking the alliteration.

He was a changed man. Approval of senior family members who had once accused him of bringing disrepute to the family name might have meant more had he changed his lifestyle out of choice. His public face had changed, his life had changed, but had he? Deep down wasn't he still the same selfish bastard he had always been? Take today and the English mouse—he had outsourced her to his cousin without a second thought, but the world thought he was a responsible, upright and valued member of society.

His lips twisted into a parody of a smile in response to the kick of self-loathing in his belly. *Because isn't that what matters?* he thought to himself.

His smile died, but the tired lines bracketing his mouth remained as his lean face set in a cynical expression, which was in danger of becoming permanently engrained. The fact was he didn't give a damn what anyone thought of him. He wasn't out to garner good opinion. The only thing he wanted, the thing his entire life focused on, was seeing his sister walk again.

He strode on, his lean face set in lines of steely determination now as he pushed aside the guilt that was a distraction and an indulgence.

Leaving the keys in the low-slung sports car—the security on the estate was good—he cut through the avenue of cedars, glad to feel the soft evening air on his face. He'd been cooped up in an air-conditioned office half the day and well into the evening. Dinner had been more about securing a contract than socialising so it had been annoying that the senior manager of the firm he was dealing with had not seemed to realise this and had brought his wife along, which had meant the meal had dragged on and no decisions had been reached.

Maybe that wasn't just due to the presence of the charming wife, though. Danilo had allowed himself to be distracted today by the thought of a pair of big, scared, golden eyes.

Those damned eyes had been prodding his conscience all day and he resented it. Hiring the Englishwoman was one of those ideas that had seemed good at the time. It was only when you walked away that you saw the flaws. If he was honest, Danilo had been hoping that Tess would get cold feet. He'd *expected* her to get cold feet but inconveniently she hadn't so presumably she was in her room now, feeling lost and overawed by her surroundings, totally out of her depth.

He just hoped that Nat hadn't been too *off* with her. He really hadn't anticipated his sister's reaction. In retrospect he could see he'd been clumsy with the way he'd broached the subject of the new, if temporary, addition to their household. The car crash of a conversation drifted through his head as he let himself into the house.

'A companion?'

He hadn't immediately recognised the danger in Nat's tone. 'More a friend.'

'Do you think I'm so pathetic you have to buy me friends? You can't buy friends.'

'I'm not—'

'Do you think I'm so stupid that I can't see what you're trying to do? She's a guard dog, isn't she? A spy—your spy—reporting back to you. I agreed not to see Marco—do you really trust me so little?'

'I do trust you, Nat,' he'd promised while thinking, *no*, it was the kid she'd got involved with he didn't trust. And Nat's reaction earlier today was yet another example of the influence the boy had had on his sweet little sister, who would never previously have argued with him this way.

He'd hardened his heart against the tears on her face and the crack in her voice when she'd said the lad's name; he'd had no hesitation in dismissing him and his decision had been proved right. Not that his sister had seemed to care when he'd revealed her boyfriend had already had several run-ins with the law.

Her reaction—*I know about that; we have no secrets*—had really set the danger bells in his head ringing.

'If this woman doesn't work out, fine,' he'd soothed, trying to make up lost ground.

'Do you even know her name?'

'She is called Tess.'

Going over the conversation in his head now, Danilo swore. He hated scenes and it was rare for Nat to treat him to one, but she had changed and he didn't know how to deal with it.

Oh, well, at least he didn't have to deal with it tonight.

He was approaching the staircase, a monumental curved cantilevered structure that was illuminated by light set in the stained-glass cupola two storeys above, when the laugh derailed his depressing train of thought. It was an unrestrained husky sound. He paused and listened, aware as he did so of the sound of music and voices, then that laugh again.

'Damn you, Franco, I meant it!' he growled as he realised this was a repeat of the night when Franco had brought back a group of friends. On that occasion they'd managed to leave a trail of destruction behind, along with the half-dressed blonde Danilo had found fast asleep on the library floor.

A dishevelled and very hungover Franco had been suitably contrite after he had first sulkily thrown the accusation of jealousy at Danilo. His jaw tightened as he moved through the rooms searching out the party venue, knowing he had no choice but to follow through with his threat of sacking Franco—an action which would no doubt bring Franco's doting mother down on his head.

'You idiot, Franco, why do you always have to push it?'

He swore softly in two languages. He'd cut Franco a lot of slack but he'd made it clear after the last incident that the next time it happened would be the last.

It wasn't until he had opened and slammed

several doors that Danilo realised the noise that he had assumed was a party in progress was actually coming from the cinema room in the basement.

Some of the tension slid from his shoulders; he smiled at his mistake.

The cinema room was one of those things that had seemed like a good idea at the time. He could count on the fingers of one hand how many times they had used it even though he'd had it installed at the same time the builders had been making the necessary adaptations to make the historical building suitable for a wheelchair, two years ago now.

The half-open door of the soundproofed room explained the noise. As he pushed it and stepped inside the noise got louder and so did the voices.

Against the background of the big screen that seemed to be playing the closing credits of an old black-and-white movie, three people sat in a half-circle.

His eyes went immediately to his sister's wheelchair, drawn up beside a table that bore the remains of a bowl of popcorn. Looking at her carefree smile brought a tightness to his chest. It made him realise how long it was since he'd seen her look that way. It reminded him of a time… He looked away quickly before the pressure in his chest became crushing, moving his focus onto Franco. His young cousin was sitting on the floor, a bottle of beer in his hand, for once not trying to look like something out of a men's fashion magazine as he took a swallow then choked, spluttering unattractively as he let out a cry of protest as the third person in the room lobbed a handful of popcorn at him.

'You pig, Franco!' His sister sent a second handful of popcorn that made her cousin duck his head.

Danilo caught himself grinning, then stopped suddenly, feeling old, or at least like the only adult in the room, but then he probably was! His interest shifted to the stranger who was curled up, her face turned away from him, on one of the big leather sofas that faced the screen with her legs tucked up under her. It was hard to tell from this angle if the person for whose benefit he assumed the conversation was being conducted in English was eighteen or thirty-eight. Franco was going through an *older* woman stage just now!

With more curiosity than he usually felt for the women in his cousin's life—this one had made his sister smile—his gaze travelled from the flash of pink-painted toenails, moving upwards over what he could see of her slim, denim-clad legs and the tee shirt she wore tucked in at the waist. The logo emblazoned across the white cotton encouraged readers to save a tree but Danilo's attention was less captured by the sentiment than the soft curves the cotton hinted at.

His libido gave a lazy kick. He recognised this as a call to stop putting off pencilling in a space in his mental diary for some fun or at least sex, because the day he felt even vaguely attracted to anyone his cousin dated it was time to take action!

As he watched her, the girl's head fell back and her face, hidden up until this point, was revealed. First just her profile, clear cut and youthful, then, as she twisted around a little, he got the full-face effect.

She was beautiful, or was that striking? A hard call to make even if his brain had been functioning, which it wasn't. The impact of that first glimpse had suspended all but the most basic functions. It took him several suspended heartbeats to wrestle it into submission and the effort brought a sheen of moisture to his skin.

He was back in control now, but struggling

to get to grips with the sheer mind-numbing strength of that flash flood of raw lust that had ribboned like fiery threads through his body. The feeling remained but in a more manageable form, a knot of pulsing desire. As he continued to stare the cause of the electrifying moment pulled her knees up to her chin and, one arm curved in a graceful arc above her head, gave a rich chuckle of laughter, low and husky. Earlier, the earthy sound had drawn him; closer up it had a nerve-tingling, tactile quality.

He had no idea what she was laughing at. It didn't really matter—the sound was genuinely infectious. The corners of his own mouth lifted as he listened to the warm and uninhibited sound.

He was still smiling as she lowered her arm and pushed a gleaming strand of the wavy golden-brown hair that fell in ripples down her back from her face while simultaneously pulling herself upright into a cross-legged sitting position. Both actions held a supple fluidity that was fascinating to watch. He studied her face, which was the visual equivalent of the uninhibited musical laughter, laughter that had a skin-tingling quality—as did that mouth!

Danilo felt the last remnants of the fatigue

that he had felt lift as he gazed at the bold, passionate curve of her lips. Fighting the fascination the pink cushiony softness exerted on him, it took a few moments to drag his gaze free from them and take in the smooth curve of high cheeks, a pointy, stubborn chin and dark slanted brows angled above wide eyes. A fractional turn of her head brought him into direct contact with those eyes, revealing a startlingly golden gaze, the amber glow emphasised by the dark rim around the iris.

The colour triggered a buried memory, where had he seen...? He shrugged away the half-formed question. No matter how deeply buried, he wouldn't have forgotten a woman this striking, this sleek and sexy.

And sensual, he silently added as he watched the tilted heavy-lidded eyes widen... in recognition? Again the question surfaced in Danilo's head but he barely heard it above the blood pounding in his skull, sending testosterone-fuelled heat flooding through his hardening body.

Not in his hormone-fuelled teens, or his hedonistic playboy days, could he recall feeling anything even approaching the level of raw sexual attraction that had nailed him to the spot for the second time in as many minutes.

He didn't have a clue how long he remained that way before he became aware of his dog nudging his leg with her nose.

Spell broken, he glanced down at the retriever at his feet, her devoted eyes on him, her tail thudding on the floor.

'Danilo!' They had parted on poor terms but his sister sounded happy to see him.

'Good girl.' He bent down to pat Goldie, offering her the treat he always carried in his pocket and letting her take it off his hand before responding to his sister's warm welcome. He continued to be aware, very aware, of Franco's date, but his social mask was fully functioning.

From his position on the floor Franco yelled, 'I want it on record that it was not my choice of film and my eyes were only watering.' With a grunt he got to his feet and held out a hand to the girl on the sofa.

She didn't need it.

She performed the action a lot more stylishly than his cousin, rising from her cross-legged pose with the natural grace he associated with a dancer. There was something about her that made him think of a Degas painting.

Something… He stopped dead, shock colliding with disbelief in his head. It was quite impossible, and for several stunned heartbeats Danilo's brain simply refused to accept it. Finally he had no choice. The proof was there in a wide-eyed amber stare that seemed to mock him.

The barefooted, glowing woman standing shoulder height to his cousin with the rippling mass of shiny hair, arrestingly vivid face and provocative dancer's body calmly returning his scrutiny was the red-nosed, needy creature who'd dragged a chivalrous response from him a week ago.

CHAPTER FOUR

THE GUILTY IMAGE of a lost, vulnerable creature rose up to mock him before vanishing. And in her place stood a woman straight from a man's sexual fantasy—or was that just his?

She dropped down into a crouch with unstudied feline grace to rub the ears of the animal who was staring up at her with longing before planting a wet doggy kiss on her nose.

'Goldie!' Danilo said sharply.

He watched, hot colour streaking his cheekbones, as Tess rose with balletic grace, rubbing her hands over invisible creases in the jeans that clung to her hips as she pulled herself up to her full height, which couldn't be much more than five-two. Her height was the *only* thing that had remained unchanged.

It *was* her, but he still couldn't believe it!

'I don't mind. She's a lovely dog,' Tess said. 'I always wanted one growing up, but my mum hates dog hairs on her clothes.'

A faithless hound, Danilo thought as the animal reacted with obvious reluctance to the click of his fingers and began to pad across the room to him.

While Danilo waited for the animal to reach him the conflicting emotions in his chest built and built until finally solidifying into something he could deal with—anger!

He'd spent the day feeling guilty for, as he'd seen it, taking advantage of the woman, for pretending even to himself that his motives were altruistic. If he'd really wanted to help Tess, he'd have dragged her to the police or even reported the incident himself, not brought her somewhere the little mouse was bound to be unhappy and out of her depth.

Yet here Tess was, in his home, looking not out of place but relaxed, as if she belonged! The roles were reversed: *he* was the one who felt like a damned intruder, an intruder in his own home, he decided, feeding his sense of outrage.

'Good evening, Mr Raphael.' She smiled and pushed her far-from-lank hair off her face. Nothing in her manner suggested she needed looking after, certainly not carrying up the stairs. Though if she had he couldn't imagine there would be any lack of offers. In fact, if you looked at the situation from one angle this might, at least on the surface, have worked out better than he could have hoped, but Danilo just couldn't shake off that initial gut response, the feeling, the totally *irrational* feeling, that he had been cheated.

'Good evening. I hope you had a good flight, Miss Jones?'

Was every dialogue she had with him going to sound like something from a Jane Austen novel? Tess wondered, deciding to go along with the lie that he had known who she was from the outset. He'd been as shocked by her appearance as she had anticipated, but she'd not been in a position to enjoy it.

Before delivering her response she pressed a hand to cover the pulse that was still frantically beating at the base of her throat. *Focus on the positive, Tess, you didn't fall down, or drool.* 'Apart from the take-off and the landing it was perfect, thank you, Mr Raphael.'

He gave an uninterested nod and continued to look every inch the brooding hero, though a lot more Heathcliff than Mr Darcy.

His sister spun her chair around and sped across the room to him, no visible trace of the sulky, resentful young woman he had seen earlier that day. He had no idea how the change had been wrought in such a short space of time, he just wished that he'd been the one responsible for it.

'Come on,' Nat urged. 'Join us. We could watch another film.'

'It's after twelve.' Danilo watched his sister's face fall, silently kicking himself when her happy smile vanished and was replaced by an antagonistic expression.

'But I'm not a child, Danilo, and, unless you've moved the goalposts, I don't have a curfew.'

Tess's elaborate and loud yawn broke the tense silence, and as eyes swivelled her way she gave a rueful grimace and apologised. 'It's been a long day. I think if nobody minds I'm ready for my bed.'

'Do you remember the way or shall I show you to your room?'

'I'm sure Miss Jones is capable of finding her own way to her room, Franco.' Danilo wondered at what point his cousin had abandoned his *dump and run* policy. Probably after the first smile. 'But first a word, Miss Jones…?' He aimed his glance a safe inch or so to the right of her lovely face, but found his eyes irresistibly tugged towards her mouth.

His inability to fight the draw of the sensual outline fanned the flame of his growing sense of being the victim of some giant con. He felt like someone who had paid for a safe and solid family car and been conned into leaving the showroom with a powerful motorbike. Shiny, attractive, guaranteed to make his heart beat faster, but not what he'd signed up for. This woman was not what he had signed up for.

His sister, framed in the doorway in her chair, swung back. 'You can't call Tess "Miss Jones" like that. It's so stuffy.'

Tess was quite happy if relations between herself and Danilo remained stuffy! Far less distracting that way!

It had taken Tess about five minutes after arriving to pick up on the underlying resentment when Natalia spoke of her brother, but it was equally obvious she adored him. It didn't take a genius to see that the household's personal dynamics were strained and she was starting to see why. Danilo had the rare ability to walk into a room and drain the joy out of it.

'Your brother is my boss, Nat.' *For how long?* was the question. His attitude suggested she had messed up in his eyes before she had even opened her mouth, or she might be paranoid.

Tess slid a covert sideways glance under her lashes towards the tall figure, and her stomach sank a little farther. No, *not* paranoid! She could feel the waves of disapproval and antagonism rolling off him from across the room, a reality that made little or no sense but then, after *that* moment tonight when she had first seen him, her reasoning capacity was pretty limited.

A little shiver rose from her toes. *Before* she had turned her head she'd known he was there. She had felt his eyes, something she had previously heard people say and she wanted to roll her eyes, but she really had!

There was no time to analyse it now, which she was quite glad about. *Disturbing* didn't begin to describe the head-spinning, finger-in-a-socket moment when heat had sizzled through her body. She had breathed her way through it and not done anything crazy but it remained a shameful reminder in her core.

There *should* have been no shock involved. She'd spent the last two hours glancing at the door, imagining Danilo standing there, at intervals glancing casually over her shoulder.

The only shock she'd anticipated, if she was honest, was *his*.

She was well aware that the last time their

paths had crossed she had rarely registered on his radar as a woman, let alone a passably attractive one. Her efforts tonight to repair the minor dent he had delivered to her ego had worked, but seriously, oh, *wow*, had they backfired!

She inhaled, living a second time through that mind-blowing moment when their eyes had connected. The heat that had flashed along her nerve endings had meant that when the anticipated recognition finally came Tess had barely registered it, let alone taken any form of satisfaction from it.

She pressed a hand to the pulse still beating frantically at the base of her throat. It had been like watching her knee jump after someone struck the right spot with a patella hammer, a reflex she had no control over. Danilo Raphael's dark stare had touched a spot, one Tess hadn't even known she had, and the resultant electrical charge that zinged along her nerve endings had been equally outside her control. Not an experience she enjoyed.

She might have been more prepared for this *weirdness* if she hadn't, up until now, worked on the assumption that everything about that evening had been exaggerated by fear and the flu—only it hadn't! If anything, her memory had downplayed Danilo Raphael. He was darker, taller; her memory recalled a man who was obviously better looking than, in her opinion, any man had a right to be, but it had not accurately recorded the innate, earthy sensuality he projected.

'No, he just writes the cheques,' she heard Natalia rebut, and dragged her attention back to the pretty young woman in the wheelchair. 'You work for me and I say it's Tess.' She angled a look that was half teasing, half challenging across the room at her brother.

'The trick, Nat,' Tess explained, 'is letting a man think it's his idea.'

It was *my idea*, Danilo thought grimly. *I brought this woman here*...and she was already creating ripples.

'We can leave the discussion until the morning if you prefer, Miss… Tess?' Perhaps recognising the coldness of his words or picking up on his cousin's puzzled looks, he added, 'I hope you had a good journey and Franco—'

'Great journey,' she cut in. The effort of smiling was starting to make her jaw ache. 'And everyone has been very kind and so welcoming.' *Until now!* 'And I'd prefer to get it over with now.' Flushing at the implication left by her words, she hastily tried to soften her comment by adding, 'That is, you're very kind, Mr Raphael, but I'm fine to talk…so long as you don't read anything into the odd yawn.' She turned towards Nat and smiled. 'See you in the morning. Goodnight, Franco. Admit it, you enjoyed the film.'

'I might have,' Franco conceded, reacting to the teasing light in her eyes with an enigmatic look that morphed into a grin as he went on to explain, 'But if I admitted that I'd have to kill you to save my reputation. *Buono notte*, Tess, it was a great night.' He gave her a hug, nodded in the direction of the tall, brooding presence of his cousin and left, closing the door behind him.

The sound threatened to trigger a nervous meltdown in Tess. Without anyone else around to dissipate it, the tangible physical charge Danilo exuded took on the form of an electrical buzz in the air. It seemed amazing that the last time she'd been alone with him she hadn't really registered it. Even more amazing was the fact his presence had made her feel safe and secure that night. She was starting to realise that that had been a one-off!

'Alone at last.' She winced as her nerves found an outlet in flippancy.

He didn't react. 'Take a seat, Miss Jones.'

Her eyes widened in a flicker of dismay. 'Why? Is this going to take long, Mr Raph...?' She left the retaliatory addition unfinished; one of them had to be a grown-up and it didn't look as if it was going to be him. 'Thanks but I feel like I've been sitting all day.'

'So how long are we to have the pleasure of your company?'

His tone was perfectly polite but somehow he managed to send the strong impression that five minutes would be too long. Tess fought the urge to ask him just what the hell she had done wrong and replied evenly.

'Your PA seemed to think me going back a week before the next school term starts would be all right. Is it?'

Danilo paused, thought of his sister's laughing face and tipped his head, unable to bring himself to ask how she had magicked the transformation in his sister he'd observed. 'You seem to be getting on well with Natalia?'

Tess ignored the fact his comment sounded more like an accusation than a compliment and responded with perfect honesty. 'That's not a big ask. Nat is a lovely girl. You must be so proud of her.'

'She tires easily.' He frowned because it sounded as if he was putting up obstacles, then continued to because he was!

'Helena filled me in on the basics.'

His glance, defying his fractured self-control, had begun to slide down her body but the mention of his PA brought his gaze back to her face.

'So what else did Helena fill you in on?'

'Not a lot. She mentioned the car accident. Though you'd already told me a bit about it. How it robbed you of your parents.' Did the perfect tailoring hide scars from the same incident? Did that explain his touchy reaction? Survivor's guilt? Or was his body marked by the tragedy that had put his sister in a wheelchair? It was the stab of painful empathy that speared through her that pushed Tess to question, 'Were you in the car?' She bit her lip, her eyes widening in dismay the moment the words were out. 'Sorry, that is none of my business.'

He elevated a dark sardonic brow, fooled not a jot by the down-bent head. She was about as meek as a tsunami! 'I am none of your business.'

She nodded, acknowledging she'd been firmly put in her place.

'But, no, I was not in the car. I was out of the country.'

His voice was flat. Too flat, she decided, wondering what nerve she had touched before she reminded herself that it was none of her business.

'If you're worried I'm too ancient to connect with your sister you shouldn't be. I can just about remember what it was like to be nineteen.'

'But you can't remember what it was like to be in a wheelchair,' he fired back, angry because that *hadn't* been his first thought. His first thought when she'd mentioned her age, typically selfish, had been that she was not too young for him.

Not that he was going to do anything about it, not while she was under his roof anyway. He might not have deliberately compartmentalised his life but it had happened and the results spoke for themselves.

'No, obviously not.'

'Of all the frustrations it involves, of having the life, the future you had planned torn away from you.'

The suddenness of it, the painful strength

of the emotions that poured off Danilo, made her take an involuntary step back from him.

He might doubt her ability to emote but Tess no longer doubted his. She felt a stab of guilt, realising that she had been on the brink of labelling him an unimaginative, control-freak bully.

'I don't suppose that any of us can, but we can try…?'

Her soft response brought his haunted stare back to her face. 'I would change places with her in a heartbeat if I could.'

He had thought it so many times but never voiced it so why the hell had he now? He lowered his eyelids to conceal his struggle as he reasserted control.

'She would probably feel the same way if the roles were reversed.'

Danilo's jaw clenched as he fought the urge to lash out at her verbally.

'But,' he said, enunciating each word slowly, 'they are not.'

If he had to lose it, why had he done so in front of this woman, who seemed to be a bottomless well of teeth-aching understanding?

He had raised his barriers so completely that if she hadn't witnessed the moment with her own eyes Tess wouldn't have believed it had happened, but it had and she'd seen something of Danilo that he hid from the world. He'd probably never forgive her for that.

'So, your duties…'

'Duties?' she echoed. She hadn't been expecting that but she was fine with it; she could multitask with the best of them. She supposed that was how rich people stayed that way: they got value for money. Besides, busy was good. It stopped her thinking about what waited for her at home, the issues that being here was delaying not resolving.

'I worked for a housekeeping agency when I was at college and—'

'You think this interests me why, exactly?' he drawled.

'Well, if you want me to work some hours in the house or garden as well—'

He looked at her as though she was speaking a foreign language, which of course she was, though that was easy to forget in a household where virtually everyone she had met spoke excellent English.

When Danilo finally realised what she was talking about he gave a thin, scornful smile. 'I do not require you to scrub floors. We have staff for that. I am speaking of what I expect of you in regard to your duties for my sister.'

Embarrassed colour flooded Tess's face as she gnawed down on her lip, unwittingly drawing his gaze to the pink fullness.

'I misunderstood.' And felt pretty stupid. 'I guess I haven't got my head into the *palace* frame of mind yet.'

'Well, let's hope we have no more misunderstandings.'

Was she imagining things or had that been a warning? Maybe not. She was getting the impression that Danilo Raphael didn't give his victims warnings—he went straight for the jugular.

Her hand lifted to her exposed neck but the shiver that went through her wasn't fear.

'My sister recently had a…'

He paused and Tess, who had given a guilty start when he started speaking, adopted an attentive expression, pushing away the lingering image of his lips brushing her neck.

'There was,' he continued slowly, 'a…' He lifted his hands in a kind of *to hell with it* gesture and finished his explanation with an impatient rush. 'She's just split up with her boyfriend.' It went against the grain to call the kid that but it got his point across, which was the main thing, without going into detail.

And it did: the sympathy on Tess's face

was instantaneous. 'Tough. Was it…' she hesitated to ask if Natalia had been dumped '…*her* idea?'

'No, it was my idea. The boy took advantage of her vulnerability to insinuate…' His jaw clenched as his anger threatened to resurface. 'He was bad news. He already had a criminal record. I was prepared to give him a chance but he abused my trust.'

'He works here?'

'He worked here,' Danilo corrected grimly.

'So your sister was all right with you sending him away?'

His glance dropped, the dark lashes that framed his incredible eyes hiding his expression momentarily. Tess was quite glad of a moment's release from that compelling dark stare.

'She will appreciate her lucky escape, in time.' And he was realising the absurdity of his compulsion to defend his actions right now. 'And in the meantime I would appreciate it if you informed me if this boy or any others try to—'

Tess held up her hand to stem the forceful flow of his words. 'Are you asking me to spy on your sister?'

His dark brows twitched into an irritated

straight line above his masterful nose. 'I wouldn't call it that.'

'Well, I would,' she exclaimed. 'And the idea makes me uncomfortable.'

A look of astonishment crossed his lean features. 'You are saying you won't?' Such an eventuality had not even crossed his mind, any more than it would cross his mind that any employee would turn around and say no when he gave an instruction.

Her chin lifted, the gleam in her eyes contrasted with her calm delivery. 'That's right.'

'The boy abused my trust.'

'And I'd be abusing Natalia's trust if I agreed to do what you want. And maybe you shouldn't push it?' she ventured.

He sucked in an astonished breath. *She* was offering *him* advice? *'Push it?'*

'Quit while you're ahead?' she offered by way of further explanation. The moment the words had left her lips, even without his rapidly darkening expression, she knew she had gone too far, but for some reason she just couldn't stop herself. The words just kept coming! 'I mean, there are not many girls of Natalia's age who would accept their brother deciding who they should or shouldn't date.

I wouldn't have…if I'd had a brother…which obviously I don't.'

'If you had a brother to watch out for you perhaps you wouldn't have to rely on a stranger to rescue you from your poor choice of men.'

His words were chosen to deliver the maximum hurt and when they clearly hit home Danilo promptly felt like an utter heel.

Even the reasonable defence that Tess could not expect to censure him that way and expect him not to retaliate did not lessen his level of guilt.

She probably didn't even think she'd done anything wrong; she was *just being honest*! It was a justification that never failed to make him see red.

He stared at her quivering lips and wondered how it was possible to want to throttle a woman one moment and comfort her the next.

Danilo did neither, but sitting on the fence was not a natural position for him. He had a black-and-white attitude to life. A decision was either right or wrong, a person someone he wanted to know or one to be avoided. A woman was one he desired or one who would drive him insane. Yet Tess Jones combined both in one small exquisite package!

'I did not choose him,' she quivered out finally. 'And before you remind me, I know that running away is never the answer but this will give me breathing space,' she added, clearly dealing with the subject before he used it as another offensive weapon.

'I wasn't going to say that, and I know what I did say was untrue, and for that I apologise.' Even after the rare *mea culpa* moment he continued to feel as guilty as hell. 'And if there is any help or legal advice whatsoever I can offer you to resolve your *problem* at home—'

Tess was totally thrown by the unexpected apology. Nevertheless she had to make it clear to Danilo that she wasn't about to be pushed around by him, any more than she wanted to be intimidated by Ben. 'I prefer to resolve my own problems my way,' she announced as though she had it all worked out.

'Fair enough.'

But he wasn't being fair. He'd been anything but! *So tell him, don't just stand there taking it*, the impatient voice in her head urged.

'Ever since you arrived I get the impression… Look, have I done something wrong? Broken some rule, kept Nat up too late? It was light beer and she is over eighteen. It's not my imagination, is it? You've been looking at me as though…as though I was a fraud. I understand that I'm not what you expected—or probably wanted.'

'I do not think you are a fraud.' He wasn't going near the wanting…the *wanting* was the problem! He couldn't look at her mouth without *wanting* to taste it. To feel her under him…

'If you're going to sack me I'd prefer you told me now, not kept me on as some sort of charity case.'

He dragged his eyes upwards.

'Do you want to leave?'

Did he want her to say yes or no? Danilo had no patience with people who did not know their own mind so recognising the ambivalence of his feelings drew a furrow in his brow.

'I like Natalia.'

The furrow smoothed.

'And I think I can be good for her.'

It wasn't relief he felt, just the satisfaction of having the decision made. 'I see you don't suffer from false modesty, but how about we give it a trial week?'

She tilted her head to one side and looked up at him, a half-smile tugging at her lips. The speed with which she had recovered amazed him. Most women he knew liked to drag out an argument until they had forgotten what it was about.

'Fine, I'll let you know if you pass the trial.'

The door had closed behind her before Danilo allowed himself to laugh.

CHAPTER FIVE

'FRANCO IS TAKING us out for a drink.'

'That's nice of him.' Nat sounded casual, but…? Tess had been here a week now. Long enough to recognise some signals. She angled a curious look at Natalia's face, wondering what she was missing this time. 'Does Franco know?'

The question drew a slightly forced laugh that suggested Tess's first instinct was right. 'Not yet,' Natalia admitted. 'But you've been here a week and it's time we showed you the action in Castelnuovo di Val di Cecina.'

'I already have,' Tess reminded Nat. She had been enchanted by the nearest small town to the estate, which itself was about midway between Florence and Pisa. It was a charming, picture-perfect medieval town surrounded by a forest of chestnut trees. Their visit had been short but she could have spent the day wandering the cobbled streets, catching glimpses of the valley below.

'At night it becomes a different place. Well, not really,' she added, with a grin. 'But there is this very nice bar. Danilo takes me there for lunch sometimes because it's so nice.'

'Franco might have other plans.'

'He might but he'll change them. He'll jump at the chance to take you out even if he has to bring me too. You must have noticed that he's got a crush on you?'

Tess had noticed but she thought it was harmless with a shelf life, she suspected, of a few days. Her half-smile faded, but what would happen if his cousin got the wrong idea? What if Danilo thought that she was encouraging Franco, or even using Franco to try to make Danilo feel jealous? *What are you doing, Tess?*

Tess brought the inner dialogue to an abrupt halt. There was a trap and she recognised it, which meant it was one dark hole she was not about to leap into. Oh, sure, she had observed how eager everyone was to defer to Danilo to change plans, but even while she felt removed from this collective rush for approval she had some sympathy.

Because despite his arrogance—or was that

because of it?—and the ruthlessness that was often only just below the surface, Danilo could also be charming, when he wanted to be, and then there was his smile, which was knockout, and his charisma was off the scale!

Her immunity to the *please Danilo* disease had made her feel a little smug, but maybe this was how it happened? How did the medical books term it...*an insidious onset*?

Her chin lifted, concern slipping into her eyes when her amused laugh wouldn't come. She had never pretended to be something she wasn't for any man and she was not going to start now!

The wattage of her smile increased. 'Do I need to change?' She glanced down. It was the sixth night she had spent at the *palazzo* and the entire dressing-for-dinner thing was still new to her. She had assumed that as staff she would be eating in the kitchen or at least in her room but Nat had made it clear that this was not the case.

The first night, spent with Franco and Nat, dinner had been a relaxed affair, but the next... well, she could tell from the way Danilo had kept staring at her bare legs that she'd got it wrong.

The next night her skirt had been even

shorter...to emphasise a point. Should the fact she felt the need to have worried her? Tess pushed away the thought. Even if she had it wouldn't have mattered: Danilo had not joined them for dinner that night or any since.

So she had dressed to please herself, quite enjoying the nightly ritual. Tonight she wore a simple, floaty, summer dress.

'You look great.'

'And if I may say so, so do you.' It was true. Nat was wearing a figure-hugging number in baby-blue silk that brought out the colour of her eyes and emphasised the voluptuous curves that Tess so envied.

There was plenty of room, but Alexandra was sitting close enough for their thighs to touch, not that many men would have complained. The designer—her company had been awarded the contract to furnish the latest luxury cruise ship that was being added to the expanding Raphael Cruise Line—looked exactly what she was: an ex-model. Topping six feet in her heels, she was slim with endless legs. Somewhat cynically he suspected that she already had her plastic surgeon of choice on speed dial for the day she didn't like what she saw when she looked in the mirror.

The rows of gold bracelets on her wrist jingled as she leaned across the table to top up her glass, giving him a free view of her excellent cleavage. Mildly amused by the action—Alex was pulling out all the stops tonight—Danilo felt his half-smile fade. Whatever Alex tried, it wasn't working.

Maybe he shouldn't have made the trip to Pisa with her. Nor suggested she break the trip from Florence to Pisa here—the small town where he was instantly recognised lacked the comfortable anonymity he sought. But why require anonymity? It wasn't as if he were committing a crime!

He considered drinking the untouched wine in his glass. Since when had he needed alcohol to appreciate a sexy woman? He held his hand above his glass as she lifted the bottle, which was now two thirds empty, not that Alex was anywhere near drunk.

'How many times a day do you need to shave? Not that I'm complaining! I like a man to look like a man.'

She lifted a hand to his cheek, rubbing her fingers across the stubble. She was a beautiful woman, at least he'd always thought so, who had made it clear on their first meeting that she was available. She'd made the first move and waited for him to make the next. He doubted she'd lost any sleep when he hadn't—until tonight.

He saw her looking at him expectantly but it was only when he took hold of her hand and placed it on the table that he realised she'd said something and he'd missed it.

'Sorry?'

'I said are you ready to leave? I don't want to keep you up too late.'

She was gorgeous and he was badly in need of sex so the question was, why wasn't he leaping to his feet and paying the cheque? This was *exactly* what he needed.

Alex leant back in her seat with a sigh. 'It's not happening for you?'

'I'm finding it hard to switch off at the moment,' he explained, unable to get the image of a pair of golden eyes out of his head.

'Don't worry, I won't take it personally.' Alex smiled and broke the connection of their thighs as she leaned over to kiss him. 'But just so you know what you're missing…'

He leaned back in his seat but she followed. Short of tipping her on the floor, he was going to have to sit there and take it like a man! Danilo doubted many would have sympathised with his dilemma. She was a good kisser, he recognised on an objective level. While on another, non-objective, totally irrational level he discovered that kissing one woman while thinking of another felt like cheating. Wrong word, wrong feeling and what the hell was wrong with a man just enjoying himself? And yet, wasn't he just going through the motions? Was he being *polite*?

The thoughts slid through his head while his half-opened eyes drifted across the room, scanning the occupants with a detached curiosity as he detachedly kissed her back. His eyes had made one sweep of the bar when quite suddenly they made contact with someone who was staring straight at him. His libido, dormant all night, roared into painful life.

He swore, pulled back and had half risen in his seat before he sank back down again. He swore again as the connection was broken and Tess's hair fell across her face. Belatedly remembering his companion, he turned his head.

'Sorry!'

The expression on Alex's beautiful face suggested that she *was* taking it personally and he couldn't blame her.

'It's just that my sister and cousin are here.'

She looked slightly mollified. 'I thought, from the way you reacted, it was your wife or something.' Automatically she followed the direction of the tilt of his head. 'I take it that the woman in the wheelchair is your sister. I heard…' She broke off, looking uncomfortable, and added, 'I've met Franco, through a mutual friend.' Curiosity slid into her eyes as she studied the second woman in the group. 'Who is his new girlfriend?'

'She is not Franco's girlfriend.' The amusement in his voice sounded forced even to his own ears. He should be laughing; it was funny—weird how the images playing in his head did not make him feel like laughing. Images that involved Franco doing the things to Tess he had been imagining doing to her all week.

'Do we have to go over?'

'No.'

Alex looked pleased. 'So, who is she?'

'She is…' Recovering a little, the heat that had streaked through his body when he had half risen in his seat coalescing in his groin, he lied coolly, 'A family friend.'

Everyone's friend in a matter of days. Tess Jones had won hearts and minds; he was the only person who had not fallen under her spell.

Ever heard of denial?

'She has gorgeous hair.' Alexandra lifted a hand to her own sleek blonde head, her confident smile twisting into a spasm of annoyance when the compliment she was fishing for didn't arrive. 'Are you going to introduce me?'

'No.' Then, to soften the bluntness of his response, he added, 'I wouldn't want to cramp their style.'

Franco gave their order to the barman and, lowering his voice, added in a conversational tone, 'Don't look now but… I said don't look!'

'Danilo!' His sister jerkily turned away, the tension that Tess had sensed growing in Natalia since they'd set off for the evening crystallising into something close to panic. '*Dio*, he isn't supposed to be here. What if he sees us and comes over…? Wait, he already knows, doesn't he?'

He has already seen us, thought Tess, who didn't turn her head. She already knew he was sitting in a corner pressed up against a gorgeous blonde who had been stroking his face adoringly when they had walked in. Unlike Nat, she hadn't experienced panic when she'd seen them, just nausea. It looked as if

Danilo was not quite the workaholic his family thought, she mused sourly.

'Knows what?' Tess asked, concerned by the younger girl's pallor.

Nat shook her head, not meeting Tess's eyes. 'Nothing.'

'Actually, I think he probably knows everything. What's the word for it? *Omniscient?*'

Tess shot Franco an irritated look. 'Not helping.' She turned to Nat. 'What if he does come over?' It didn't matter; his presence had already ruined the night for Tess. 'We haven't broken any laws.' Except the unwritten one that said no one could do anything without asking him first! The man was a control freak, she decided. But her thought processes were suspended by a fresh wave of nausea as the couple on the other side of the room began to kiss.

Franco, who was watching them too, let out a low chuckle. 'I doubt if he will. It looks to me like they'll be leaving soon.' His observation was tinged with envy as he added, 'Talk about get a room.'

Tess's mind had already gone to the scene Franco's comment painted. 'Is that his girlfriend?' She was staring; she didn't want to but she couldn't stop.

Ignoring his own advice, Franco turned his head. 'Danilo doesn't have girlfriends...he just has *partners*.' He glanced down at his cousin with a grimace of apology. 'Sorry, Nat.'

'Do you really think I thought my brother was a monk?'

Not a mistake anyone who had looked at his mouth would have made! The thought materialised at exactly the moment his eyes connected with hers. A flood of mortified heat scorched through Tess's body as she looked away. He hadn't really seen her, not at that distance, it had just seemed like it—but she had been staring.

She picked up her glass of wine and willed herself not to look back, though if they didn't want people to look they should really have taken Franco's advice, she decided crossly. If anyone should be embarrassed it should be Danilo.

'I'm just going to the ladies' room,' Nat announced, swivelling her lightweight chair around.

'Hold on.' Tess moved to walk beside the chair. Her determination *not* to think about Danilo having sex, especially with the tall beautiful blonde, had the predictable result that that was pretty much *all* she could think of. 'I'll come with you.'

'No! It's fine. That's why I suggested this place. It's very wheelchair friendly.'

Tess, watching her move away, frowned. 'Has anything happened today? Natalia seems a bit distracted.'

'I thought she looked pretty good tonight.'

'Yes, I know, but don't you think—?'

'Danilo a monk? That's a laugh! Before the car accident there were lots of girls, lots of nightclubs and—'

Tess, who had seen the pictures, read the stories, cut him off. 'You mean you modelled yourself on him?'

'I wish! The *treat them mean keep them keen* thing doesn't work for me. Seriously though, since the accident he's changed.' He flashed the cool blonde a look. 'Though not in everything. She is definitely his type.'

'Look, do you mind if we talk about something that *isn't* your cousin's, and my boss's, sex life?'

She aimed for casually amused but from Franco's expression she knew she'd missed it by several shrill miles.

Before he could say anything she handed him her glass. 'I'm going to check on Nat. I'm sure something is wrong. I'll have the same again.'

'Who am I to argue with women's instinct?'

When Tess found the ladies' room it was empty but for a couple of women who were checking their already perfect make-up.

'Sorry but have you seen a woman…in a…' about to say 'blue dress', she stopped, and, re-membering a comment Nat had made about people noticing the chair and never seeing her, she finished with '…wheelchair?' The two looked blankly at her, not understanding a word, and with a frustrated grimace she shook her head. 'Never mind.'

Had she somehow missed Nat? Back out in the carpeted passageway she retraced her foot-steps, standing by the doorway so she could scan the entire room. She could see Franco at the bar where she'd left him; there was no sign of either Nat or Danilo and his blonde. Starting to get seriously worried now, she ran back towards the ladies' room. This was stu-pid. Nat had to be somewhere; she couldn't just have vanished.

As she stood there telling herself not to panic a door opened and a couple walked through. Before it closed Tess got a glimpse of a few tables spread over what appeared to be a cobbled courtyard area.

She ran towards it, and took a deep breath. If Nat wasn't here she was going to have to raise the alarm. She pushed the door open. The space behind the door was a lot smaller than it had seemed. Probably a sun trap during the daylight hours, now it was illuminated by fairy lights strung along the wooden struts of the pergola arrangement overhead. All in all the effect was romantic and intimate. The couple there obviously thought so!

'Nat!'

The couple broke apart, the young man who was squatting beside the wheelchair rocking back on his heels.

Natalia, her expression one of embarrassment mingled with defiance, shook her head and took one of the young man's hands between both of hers. 'You can't tell him!'

Tess didn't need to ask who the 'him' she was talking about was. *Oh, hell, just what she needed!*

'He'll kill Marco!' Nat pronounced dramatically.

'I don't think that it'll come to that, Nat.'

The young man got to his feet. 'I am not afraid of your brother.'

More fool you, Tess thought as he extended his hand.

'I'm Marco.'

Tess took the hand and realised she was between the proverbial rock and a very hard place. Unbidden an image of Danilo floated into her head. He was the living embodiment of hard. Hard in every sense of the word, she decided. Ashamed of the illicit shiver that trickled down her spine, she pushed the image away.

'I'm Tess.'

'She's a friend. She's on our side, aren't you, Tess?'

Her instinct told her to respond with a yes but her common sense told her that taking any *side* would be a major mistake, so she side-stepped the question.

'I take it that you didn't accidentally bump into one another?' She arched a brow and looked from one to the other. 'Which is why you panicked when you saw your brother?'

The young man's eyes widened. Tess didn't need to understand Italian to get the gist of what he was saying.

'He's gone.'

'I will protect you from him, *cara mia*.'

Nat touched his arm. 'He's not a monster, Marco.'

'You defend him?'

'No, but…he thinks I'm still a kid, and he thinks me being in this is somehow his fault.' She banged the chair with her hand. 'He won't stop looking for a miracle. I hope you won't tell him.' She gave a little sigh that tore at Tess's heart. 'But if you do, I'll understand.'

Tess really wished that Danilo could witness this display of maturity from Nat, and she *really* wished she had not discovered the young lovers' secret. This was definitely a lose-lose situation, and as much as she sympathised with the young couple she could also see where Danilo was coming from. She felt a surge of exasperation. If he hadn't waded in with his size twelves the affair would probably have died a natural death by now. There was no better fuel for young love than prohibition!

'I don't want to be part of a conspiracy of silence, but, all right, I won't tell him, but I think you should. He will find out at some point and it'll be much easier if you come clean now. Just explain to him how you feel, the way you just explained it to me.'

'You know what happened to the last person who told Danilo he was wrong?'

Tess shook her head.

Nat gave a high-pitched laugh. 'Right, because nobody does.' Without warning her anger dissolved and her eyes filled with tears. 'I love my brother and I don't want to make him unhappy, but I love Marco too.'

Tess felt a sharp stab of sympathy. She knew what it was like to try and please the person you loved and fail. For years she had tried to be the daughter her mother wanted; it was only when she'd stopped trying that she'd realised her mum loved her even if she was never going to be a political asset.

Nat's sob was cut off as the door opened and four young women in a party mood spilled out into the courtyard. The illusion of privacy vanished as their laughter and chatter filled the air.

'I think it's best if you go now, Marco.'

The young man appeared inclined to protest but Natalia backed up Tess's suggestion. 'I'll be fine.' She glanced at Tess and said defiantly, 'I'll call you tomorrow.'

CHAPTER SIX

THEY WERE BACK at the palazzo before eleven. On the journey home Natalia had closed her eyes and given a not very realistic impression of being asleep. Once they were inside, pleading a headache, Natalia announced her intention of going straight to her room.

Tess, whose own head was pounding, made sympathetic noises and managed to insert a softly spoken comment before the girl disappeared. 'You know you have to tell him, don't you? Or stop seeing Marco.'

Natalia lifted her chin and glared at Tess. 'That's up to me, isn't it, not you? I can't stop you telling Danilo but I don't have to listen to your advice, considering you're being paid to give it!' Her lips quivered and her eyes filled. 'I… I'm sorry. I know I've put you in a terrible position but I can't give him up.'

Tess stood there waiting until the sound of slamming doors stopped, but waiting for what?

To find someone I can't give up?

It hadn't happened yet.

And it never would, not while she… Tess sucked in a shocked breath through parted lips, and thought, *Not while I can carry on pretending the only men who are attracted to me are the ones that ignited nothing inside more dangerous than friendship and affection.*

Even while the echoes of this flash of insight reverberated around inside her skull, she began to push it away.

Because burying something solves it?

She set her soft jaw. This was *not* about her mum's sleazy boyfriend. He had faded away, out of their lives, and she had not asked questions, just felt relief, relief that she didn't have to tell her mum, knowing that her parent would shoulder all the blame.

But what if she'd buried the memory but not the fear? The fear of not being in control, of being helpless, went so deep that at some subconscious level she'd discouraged the attention of any man she could imagine herself losing control with.

Was all this denial now catching up with her?

Was it coincidental that she found herself

in a place she had never even dreamt existed? Feeling things she had never felt, never *wanted* to feel and unable to stop imagining herself losing control with a man who was not at all safe… Or was it fate?

The slamming of doors had interrupted Danilo's online study of the statistical breakdown of surgical success rates for the few surgeons who had so far attempted the technique that in theory could give his sister some mobility back.

He was glad of the interruption. The numbers did not make easy reading, even with a glass of brandy in his hand. He wasn't drunk but he'd had enough to blur the edges a bit and lower the volume on the uncomfortable questions circling in his head.

When, glass in hand, he went to investigate the commotion he discovered one of the questions—*or should that be one of the answers?*—standing in the hallway, her face covered by her hands. Anything approaching mellow vanished as heat streaked through his body.

He lifted the glass and over the rim took the opportunity to study Tess unobserved. Under the shield of his long dark lashes his eyes made a slow, predatory, upwards sweep from her feet, in the heels that gave her an extra three inches. She looked fresh, gorgeous and very sexy. By the time he reached her glossy head he decided he had either drunk too much or not nearly enough.

'So, a bad night, then?'

The deep drawled comment made Tess leap like a startled deer and spin around.

About a dozen doors opened off the massive marble-floored central hallway. The one that was now open led to a room Tess had never before entered: Danilo's study.

Danilo himself, looking tall, sleek and panther like, stood framed there and the rush of hormones she experienced made her head spin and her knees sag. A wave of intense longing washed like a relentless tide over her until her autonomic responses kicked in to equal the pressure building in her chest. She took a deep, shuddering breath.

'What are you doing here?' she squeaked, her voice accusingly shrill in her own ears.

'I live here.' His voice was mild; his stare was not. The dark blaze in his eyes made her stomach muscles quiver.

'I know.' Even before he reacted with a sardonic look of amusement Tess flushed and felt

stupid—she was recognising a theme here—
and as the guilty conviction took hold that he
could see into her head it was all she could do
to stop herself blurting out the secret. *Which
one?*

'Sorry.' *Act normally. He doesn't know. He
can't know, you're being paranoid.* 'You startled me.' She managed an edgy smile; if only
that were *all* he was doing to her! As if his
dark stare acted like some sort of truth drug,
she had to endure the relentless, hormonal
urge that reacted indecently to his presence.

While she was wondering if he had this
effect on all women a memory surfaced in
her head of the text she had received from
Fiona on her first night here. She'd been able
to laugh about it then; now, days later, it would
be a struggle even to raise a smile.

Well, you've met him in the flesh, so how gorgeous is he on a scale of one to ten and, more
importantly—would you?

Tess had responded in a similarly jokey
style—had it really been only six days ago?

If I said he's a fifteen he'd be the first to agree—
and, no, definitely not!

Actually, since then she had noticed Danilo was surprisingly lacking in the vanity department, possibly because he seemed to be oblivious to the way women stared at him. The other part of her response held true. She took comfort in the blatant lie and more comfort from the knowledge that she was never likely to be called upon to prove it, not when there were blondes like the one he'd been with tonight.

Pity her hormones had simply not got the message. He did look sinfully sexy standing there, one shoulder wedged against the acanthus-carved door frame, his white shirt unbuttoned at the neck, not a lot but enough to reveal a deep vee of golden skin and a smattering of darkly curling chest hair, which was too much for her comfort.

Mouth dry, heart pounding, she was simultaneously ashamed and excited. Guilt added yet another layer of discomfort to the moment. Tess dampened down a spurt of panic. If he asked her outright would she lie? More to the point *should* she lie?

Wasn't her silence as bad as lying?

Her guilt made her see suspicion in his face, the planes and strong angles emphasised by the dark stubble on his jaw and lean cheeks enhancing the fallen-angel quality of his features. As he dragged his hand back and forth across his hair she noticed that he looked heavy-eyed, as though he'd just tumbled out of bed.

Maybe he had?

Her stomach gave a deep lurch as her agile mind made another leap—or not bed, she speculated as an image of the tall blonde flashed through her thoughts, the woman's red-painted nails pressed into his hard, golden flesh.

Perhaps, she thought sickly, they hadn't made it that far?

She took a deep breath, reminded herself that Danilo Raphael's sex life was none of her business. So what if the blonde, looking less cool and more mussed than earlier, *was* behind that door stretched out on a sofa waiting for…? She pressed a hand to her stomach. A vivid imagination was at times a curse.

'Sorry to disturb you,' she mumbled, her expression determinedly composed as she stared at the intricate carving on the wall frieze to his right as though it were the most fascinating thing she had ever seen. A glimpse of some half-dressed woman was *not* a memory she wanted, though her eyes seemed to have other ideas. 'I was on my way…' She stopped. He was barefoot; in her head the detail confirmed all her suspicions.

'Is something wrong?'

'Not a thing,' she said stonily.

'I'm having a nightcap.'

She lifted her eyes from his feet and saw that Danilo was holding a drink in one hand. The amber liquid in the heavy crystal glass caught the light from the central chandelier and made her blink. She met his eyes, suddenly picking up on details she'd missed: the almost feral gleam in his half-closed, heavy-lidded eyes, the almost combustible tension in his lean body. He was like a man who had started something and...?

Her eyes widened as her imagination once more went into manic overdrive mode. Had he and the blonde argued? They'd seemed pretty friendly when she'd seen them, Tess thought sourly. Maybe the woman had a high-powered career and had been called away leaving him frustrated...drowning his sorrows? Looking for a substitute?

'Would you like to join me?'

The husky invitation brought her speculation to a dead halt, though she'd been so caught up that it took her a few moments to focus on what he'd said.

'Join...?' Her eyes moved past him to the room where she could see a ceiling-high wall of bookshelves.

'I'm inviting you for a nightcap, not to join an orgy.' He rolled the word around his tongue as though he were tasting it, seeming to take pleasure from her discomfort.

Discomfort was a massive understatement, Tess felt like a pawn and she didn't like the sensation. 'Now, there's a word you don't get to use every day.'

He arched a dark brow, a half-smile quivering. 'Nightcap?'

'You're alone?' The incautious words were out before she could censor them.

'Who do you think I have in there?' He nodded at the room behind him without taking his eyes from Tess's face.

'It isn't any of my business.'

He burst out laughing.

Tess didn't join in. It was hard when you knew you *were* the joke.

'Sorry, it's just that you look...' He paused, took a swallow of his drink and drawled, 'Like an outraged nun.' If nuns wore dresses that short! His eyes dropped to the outline of her hips and bare, smooth calves, and the ever-present lust developed claws and dug deep.

'I could feel your disapproval across the bar earlier.'

So he had seen them.

'I was simply surprised,' she managed with something that resembled cool. 'It was quite a coincidence we had… At least Nat had received the message that you were in Florence.'

'So you weren't stalking me?' He watched her expression freeze and swore, his teasing attitude vanishing in the blink of an eye as she bit down hard on her trembling lower lip. The sight of the pinpricks of blood sent his protective instincts into overdrive, shaking loose a need to comfort inside him.

'Sorry,' he roughed out, his face a mask of contrition. 'Bad choice of verb. You shouldn't worry, you know, I'm pretty sure that you'll have no problems with that guy in the future.'

His trip to Dublin two days earlier, where he had a team working around the clock to deliver a report on the viability of the plan to redevelop a derelict industrial area, had meant a stopover in London could barely be classed as an inconvenience.

The stalker, according to the detailed dossier that had landed on his desk, was a man who lived his life to a pretty rigid schedule. The 'query OCD' written in the margin had seemed a good call to Danilo—which had made locating him easy.

The rest had not been rocket science. Once he had convinced the crazy that he was dealing with someone who was actually crazier than he was, it had been easy. Fear was a great motivator.

Tess didn't share his confidence, but, unwilling to reveal just how much the situation awaiting her in London was preying on her mind, she managed a cautious, 'I hope so.' Then surprised herself by revealing a decision she had made the previous evening, but not the repeating nightmare that had inspired it. 'I might swallow my pride and ask my mum's advice when I get back.' She caught his questioning look and added, by way of explanation, 'She knows some people…'

'That sounds ominous. Should I watch my step?'

Her smile glimmered as she imagined her mother as part of a criminal gang. 'Not *those* sort of people. She has contacts, with some women's charities, among other things.'

'She sounds an interesting woman.'

'She is.'

'I am surprised you haven't called on her expertise before.'

'My mum's help comes at a price. Look, can we talk about something else?'

He lifted his brows a little at the tautness of her voice but complied with her request. 'I have noticed the change in Natalia since you arrived.'

She tensed, waiting for the invisible blade she could feel above her head to fall. Did she tell him that Nat's affair preceded her arrival or keep quiet?

'I can't remember the last time she went out.'

She had been so sure that he knew that the unexpected reprieve made her body sag with a relief that was short-lived, as she realised that the last time Nat went out was likely as not for a secret meeting with her boyfriend.

Tess didn't know for sure. She hadn't asked and she wasn't going to; she had enough secrets to guard.

'But I'm sorry you didn't have a good evening.'

'It was fine,' she lied, bringing her lashes down in a protective sweep. 'I have a headache.' That at least was not a lie.

'Well, I'm glad that you persuaded Nat to go out. However, I'd prefer it if in future you run such things past me.'

Tess stiffened at the casual addition. 'Let

me get this straight. What are you saying exactly? That when Nat suggests we go for a drive I have to say, "Hold on a moment, I just have to go ask your brother"—which, incidentally, might be hard as you're never here! Good grief, Danilo, aren't the walls here high enough without you adding more restrictions?'

His expression had grown colder as she'd been speaking and by the end of her impassioned speech his eyes were ice chips. 'Natalia is free to come and go as she pleases. I simply—'

'I'm not your sister's nursemaid and I think I made it quite clear when you made that particular suggestion before that I'm not about to act as your spy.' *That would make me a double agent.*

He made a clicking sound of aggravation with his tongue, dug his hands into his pockets and levered his long, lean length away from the wall. 'You really do have a talent for drama. I didn't ask you to be a spy.'

His attitude, the male arrogance oozing out of his every perfect pore, just touched a nerve and made her reckless. 'It's small wonder, if you treat her like a prisoner, that she doesn't feel she can discuss things with you!'

'But she discusses them with you?'

Tess's outrage dissolved like a spoonful of sugar in an ocean. She faked a smile and reminded herself that guilt was making her paranoid. But the way he was looking at her, as though he knew…but he couldn't—could he?

So, suddenly she had nothing to say for herself? While this was a pleasant change it did not lessen Danilo's anger at the accusations she'd already made. The very real possibility she might be right intensified those feelings of outrage, and left the taste of failure in his mouth.

Oh, he could shrug off the claim that Nat was afraid of him, and obviously there were things that she didn't tell him, that was normal, but he hated the distance that had grown up between them recently and he hated that he didn't know how to fix it. And if Nat hating him was the price of her walking again it was one he was willing to pay, but it did not make the prospect any more palatable.

'While I admire confidence, is it *conceivable* after what…a week here that you can be considered an expert on my relationship with my sister? But who knows?' Hands thrust into his pockets, he lifted his broad shoulders in a contemptuous shrug and sketched a smile. 'If you had run tonight's plan past me I would have been able to explain that because my sister's treatment is ongoing we are scheduled to fly to London tomorrow to see a consultant. The trip will be tiring for her and, if asked,' he drawled, 'I would have advised an early night, if of course that would have met with your approval.'

With each successive sarcastic stab from his cruel tongue Tess felt as if she were getting smaller, shrinking, so that by the time he had finished with her she'd moved beyond mortified blushes, was as pale as paper and felt about six inches tall.

'If Nat had told me——' She closed her mouth, pretty sure that ignorance would be no defence in Danilo's eyes.

'Nat doesn't know.'

She stared, too bewildered by the admission to be tactful. 'Why? Was it a last-minute thing?'

It was a toss-up which he found more aggravating: being asked to explain his actions, or feeling the need to do so. 'No. I made the arrangements before I left London.' And he was not about to question his decision; it was the right one. 'If Nat had known she would have worked herself up, become…upset…' She was still going to get tense and tearful, but at least this way she would not have spent the last week in a state of nervous anticipation.

So instead of that, Natalia had met up with her secret lover and become…upset. If Danilo had known…? Even as Tess closed down that avenue of speculation she acknowledged that, as things stood, it was inevitable that at some point she'd find out *exactly* how Danilo would react—unless Nat gave up Marco, which did not seem likely.

'You see, while I may lack your expertise, *I* have done this before and I do know my sister.'

Not as well as you think. 'So you'll tell Nat tomorrow.'

He nodded. 'The appointment is in the afternoon.'

'How long will Natalia be in London?' And what, Tess wondered, was she meant to be doing while the woman she was being paid to be a companion to took a trip?

'Just overnight and it's *we*.'

Tess shrugged. She had taken it as read that Danilo would be accompanying his sister.

'Only a flying visit, it depends on what Nat wants, but we could stay overnight or fly straight back, so don't pack too much.'

'*Me?* You want me to come?'

He arched a brow and looked impatient. 'You can't be company for Nat when you're in another country.'

'So you've booked my ticket?'

He looked at her blankly and she immediately felt stupid. Unlike her own, Danilo Raphael's world did not involve last-minute bargain flights.

'Nat's physio session is when?'

'Eight-thirty.'

'I'll cancel. It might be a good idea if you were on hand…'

'To take the flak?'

'I am more than capable of taking the flak, but if you could be there to…' Head bent, he dragged a hand across his face, the gesture so revealing that Tess's heart ached.

'Just be there, I would be…' his eyes brushed hers and the pause lengthened before he added an abrupt and harsh '…grateful.'

In her head she could see the door closing with a decisive whoosh and a dismissive click and she felt something approaching panic. He couldn't go! She needed more from him.

'So what time?'

Hand on the study door handle, Danilo swung back, his stance tense as he failed to stop himself imagining a scenario where he didn't reply, he just took those two fatal steps, hauled her into him, felt the collision of her soft body into his and discovered if those lips tasted as good as they looked. They would and he would take his time, he would… The effort to drag his thoughts away from the fantasy spinning in his head drew an audible grunt of effort from his throat.

'I haven't decided yet.'

The door closed.

Hands clenched, she turned away. *How pathetic are you, Tess?*

The answer, disturbingly, was that where Danilo Raphael was concerned—very!

She discovered the next day just how different travelling Raphael style was when they had boarded the private jet. Natalia took the luxury for granted, but it reduced Tess to a state of wide-eyed wonder, which she pushed to one side as she attempted to make conversation with Natalia. She managed to coax a smile or two out of the other woman but in the end, despite all her efforts to distract her, she lapsed into moody silence.

Distracting hadn't worked so Tess decided to face the elephant in the room. It turned out not quite as she hoped.

'You must be excited.'

'Excited?'

'About the appointment, the possibility—'

'That I'll walk again? There have been other appointments, a lot of them, there will be more. Danilo will never give up. He believes in miracles.'

Tess's throat had closed up with emotion. Natalia's dry eyes, the bleak acceptance in her voice, was more affecting than floods of tears could ever have been.

The helplessness she was feeling, she realised, was something that Danilo must feel every day, only magnified by a thousand.

The limo that took them from the airport continued the style of travelling, which, if she was honest, Tess could easily become accustomed to. Not that she would have the opportunity. In a few weeks she would be making the same journey, but on her bargain, no-frills flight. The time she had spent with the Raphaels a dim and distant memory. It was disturbing how she had become involved in the family's life during such a short period of time, but she knew that the intimacy was an illusion, that it would be a mistake to forget that she was just the hired help.

Tess enjoyed the car journey a lot less than the plane partly because during the flight she had not seen Danilo, who had been closeted away working, but there was no escaping his sheer overpowering physicality in the enclosed space. There was no escaping; the accidental brush of his knee against hers was enough to send a rush of charged hormonal heat through her body. She had never experienced anything like this before!

It seemed unlikely that a man with his experience didn't know what he did to her, which made those little things he kept doing, like staring at her mouth when they were talking, or standing too close, just plain cruel. It was equally possible that she didn't even register on his radar as a woman. She wasn't sure which scenario was preferable.

While the tension between herself and Danilo might not have existed outside her imagination, the tension between brother and sister was very real. Every glance and comment Natalia made was double-edged and loaded as she shot down in flames everything Danilo said. He must have noticed but he didn't react to any of the jibes or snapped comments. Tess actually found her sympathies swinging his way until Nat suddenly looked at him, her eyes filled with tears, and whispered a broken, *'Sorry!'*

Danilo just squeezed his sister's hand and smiled. 'It's fine.'

Tess had to look out of the window to hide the tears that she struggled to blink away, only looking back when the limo pulled to a halt.

'We're early. I thought we'd stop for tea first. This is your favourite?'

Nat looked out of the limo window at the hotel they had drawn up at. 'Lovely.' The girl's attempt to inject some enthusiasm into her dead voice brought another lump of emotion to Tess's throat.

She glanced at Danilo but the expression on his face told her nothing about what he was feeling.

An hour later, she stood in the ladies' room running her hands under the cold-water tap. The tea-time treat had been agony, but then sitting around a table with two people who barely spoke was never going to be relaxing, especially if the silence played out to a background of nerve-stretching tension.

'And you thought *you* had problems,' she told her reflection in the mirror.

She didn't want to think about her cringe-worthy efforts to fill the silences. To say she'd overcompensated was putting it mildly! She'd sounded like—the memory of the steady flow of bright chatter she'd maintained made her wince. By the end of the afternoon tea the sound of her own voice was grating on her, and none of her jollity had rubbed off on her companions.

Delaying the moment she had to go back, Tess lingered in the perfume-scented room for as long as possible, but there were only so many times a girl could reapply her lipstick.

'Time to man up, Tess,' she told herself sternly before squaring her shoulders and stepping out into the lobby.

When she had entered the space had been empty but it was now packed with people, some holding microphones, others cameras, all being aimed at an elegant figure who was fielding questions being thrown at her.

Tess stopped dead, experienced a mind-blanking rabbit-in-the-headlight moment, though fortunately she unfroze before anyone noticed her. The thought of the attention shifting her way made her shudder.

Danilo, who had been tapping his foot with impatience and contemplating invading the sanctuary of the ladies' powder room, saw that Tess was overwhelmed by the crowd she encountered in the lobby. He watched her skirt round the very edges of it, doing her best not to look up or make any eye contact.

She was so intent, for some reason, on avoiding attention and the woman who was fielding questions like the pro she clearly was, that she didn't register his presence until he touched her shoulder, at which point she jumped guiltily.

'What took so long? Nat is in the car.'

'Sorry, sorry… I…well, I'm here now.' She stepped around him so that he was between her and the public interview, his body acting as an effective shield, and she stayed that way until they had safely exited the building.

In the car she sank into her seat with a sigh and closed her eyes, though she opened them again when Danilo, sitting opposite her, said casually, 'Did you know that woman?'

'What woman?' Nat asked, looking from one to the other. 'You mean, the one in the lobby…who was she?'

'Beth Tracey. She's running for mayor.'

Tess didn't know why his knowledge surprised her. 'She hasn't actually confirmed that yet.' Maybe that was what the media scrum had been about.

'So you do know her?' Danilo pushed.

'Sort of…' He elevated a brow and she revealed with a hiss of exasperation, 'She's my mother.'

For the first time since she'd met him she saw Danilo Raphael look shocked. She supposed that was a triumph of sorts but she was used to that reaction from strangers when they discovered her parentage.

'You don't have the same name.'

Tess forced a smile to respond to Nat's observation. 'She uses her maiden name.'

'And how does your father feel about that?'

The question came from Danilo, so she turned her head to look at him. 'He died when I was small. Mum raised me as a single parent.'

'Your mum is famous…cool,' Nat pronounced. 'So don't you get on?'

Well, at least her family dynamics were proving a distraction for Natalia, who obviously found the situation curious.

'We get on fine. It's just that we are not very alike—we live very separate lives. She is very busy. I am…' She paused, thinking, *a disappointment*. 'I'm very proud of her.'

'I didn't realise that you had family in London. If you'd like to stop over and fly back tomorrow…?'

Tess was surprised by the offer. 'No, that's fine. I doubt Mum could see me at this short a notice.'

'You have to make an appointment to see your mum?'

You could see that in Nat's world this was pretty freaky and the girl's amazement made Tess wish she hadn't been quite so literal in her response.

'No, of course not,' she said, laughing off the idea. 'But she's busy campaigning at the moment.'

'And won't you be called on to help?'

After fighting the urge to announce it was not anyone's business, Tess gave a terse, tight-lipped response to Danilo's continued probing. 'Mum accepted that I'm not a political asset years ago and she has plenty of people happy to leaflet drop.'

They got to the Harley Street office a few minutes later. Tess waited in the ground-floor waiting room, which looked more like a drawing-room illustration from a glossy homes magazine, while brother and sister were escorted to the lift that took them up to the consulting rooms.

Tess refused the tea on offer, leafed through

a few magazines but eventually, as the tension built, had to get up and walk around the room. If she felt like this she could only imagine what Nat was feeling right now, and Danilo. After half an hour of pacing she made herself sit down.

Her bottom had barely touched the seat when Danilo walked in so she sprang to her feet.

It was hard to read anything in Danilo's expression. 'How—?'

'Natalia had some questions for the doctor.' It was the first time that his sister had asked for him to leave.

The expulsion had been a shock, and one he had not seen coming. For two years he had been the conduit between the medics and his sister; the rejection—and that was what it had felt like—had caught him on the raw. She was asserting her independence, he got that, he even had some sympathy with it, but the fact was he knew what questions to ask, he knew—'

Tess's voice interrupted his brooding reverie.

'*What?*'

Tess was relieved to hear him sound irritable, and even more relieved to see the blank look that had made her think the worst slide from his eyes. 'I said, did it go well?'

He flashed her a sardonic look. 'That depends on your definition of well, but it did not go badly. This was just the first consult. There will be more.' He hesitated long enough to worry her again before adding, 'I know you are scheduled to have a day off tomorrow and if you have plans that is fine, but would you mind spending some time with Nat? The days after one of these…it can be hard for her.'

And you, Tess thought, sensing the unacknowledged distress behind his closed expression and wondering if Danilo ever allowed himself a moment's weakness. She fought down the urge to say something comforting, pretty sure it would be received with as much appreciation as a spontaneous hug would have been.

'Of course I can.' Tess did have plans but they involved Natalia.

He tipped his head, aware even at this moment of a hard throb of need as their glances connected. 'I am grateful.'

She didn't want his gratitude, but she wanted to see him smile, see him happy, see the lines of tension bracketing his mouth smooth out. The strength of these feelings shocked her and made her blurt out unthinkingly, 'So, things are good right now?' The words brought his sardonic gaze to her face. 'I mean, not as bad as they could be? My mum always says you should live for the moment.' She closed her eyes and muttered, 'That sounded better in my head. I just meant—look, if you ever want to talk about—'

She was looking up at him, all earnest concern and 'a pat on the head, a cup of tea will make you feel better.' Something inside Danilo snapped. He didn't *deserve* to feel better; maybe this was him being punished? Pity from this woman with that mouth, that body— the sort that a man could fall into and forget.

Tess's eyes blinked wide when without warning his big hand curved around the back of her head, the movement almost casual as he drew her closer. Too startled to react, Tess registered the driven gleam in his heavy-lidded eyes as he lowered his head until his mouth was a whisper away from hers, their foreheads almost touching.

She held her breath, the languid weakness that spread through her body infecting every cell. Time seemed to slow, though in retrospect when she thought of the incident she realised it only lasted moments before he pulled back.

Clearing her throat, Tess struggled to regain a semblance of composure, and tried to reboot her lust-battered brain. What was she meant to do? Pretend nothing had happened? Shrug away the moment? Probably the wisest option but nobody had ever accused her of being wise.

She lifted her chin. 'So, what was that about?'

'A lesson.' For him as much as her, he decided, hugging his self-loathing tight as he reflected darkly on his supreme selfishness. His sister was facing a decision that could give her back her life or close off that possibility for ever. What sort of man could think about sex at a time like this?

The man he was.

Tess Jones might not know she needed protecting from him but Danilo did, and the simplest way to extinguish that sympathetic glow in her eyes was to open them. 'I realise that you consider *feelings* your area of expertise, but men—'

'Do not have feelings?' she suggested, starting to feel angry.

'They do not talk about them obsessively,' he sneered.

'So what *do* men do?'

'To relieve stress? Speaking for myself I

find that sex works, so unless you're offering, *cara*…?' he drawled.

Tess lowered her lashes as the carnal bluntness of his careless words sent an unexpected thrill of excitement through her. Shocked more by her response than his comment, she was trying to think of a suitable response when he continued.

'You are very curious about our lives, but not so eager to share when it comes to your own family.'

'I don't know what you mean.'

'You couldn't close down the subject of your mother fast enough.'

'That's—'

'None of my business?'

Tess flushed but was spared responding when Nat appeared.

'How—?'

Nat shook her head. 'Not now, Danilo, can we just go home…please?'

CHAPTER SEVEN

AFTER DRIVING HIS car from the helipad where he'd left it that morning, Danilo changed his mind and took a detour when he heard the distant sounds of activity coming from the direction of the indoor arena.

Change your mind? mocked the voice in his head. *Wasn't this always where you were going since you started imagining Tess in a pair of riding breeches?*

She'd caught up with him just before he'd driven off to the helipad that morning; her hair had still been wet from the shower and even though she had yelled her request from twenty feet away he had imagined he could smell the scent of her shampoo.

Twenty feet was pretty much the distance she had kept from him since the previous week's trip to London. It helped but not enough. Logic didn't enter into it so he had stopped trying to work out why, despite the fact her position in the household put her off limits. He wanted her on such a fundamental level.

Pushing away the image of her face as he walked, he slung his discarded jacket over his shoulder. The day was turning out to be another warm one. He glanced at the slim silver-banded watch on his wrist as he headed towards the building.

It was early, but freed from the relentless round of meetings for the first time in what felt like weeks he could, he had reasoned, as easily work at home this afternoon, which he would have explained to anyone who asked, not that they had. He was the boss—or, as his father would have said, the buck stopped with him.

'When that day comes, Danilo, for you to step into my shoes—' at the time he had wanted to be a fighter pilot or a rock star '—you'll understand that leadership can be lonely. You won't always know the answers, but—'

'You do.'

'Sometimes, to be a successful leader, *acting* as if you know what you're doing is as important as actually knowing, but follow your instincts, Danilo, and you won't go far wrong.'

At the time he'd been unable to get his head around the idea of his father not being omnipotent and actually winging it. As for instincts, he hadn't been very sure he had any, at least not the sort his father had been talking about.

He succeeded in pushing away the lingering echo of his father's voice but the sadness remained. That *time* his father had spoken of had come a lot sooner than either of them had expected, and Danilo hadn't stepped into his shoes but been propelled by tragic events. Others within the financial empire his father had presided over had worried about how the financial world would react to this transition, which had in the end been seamless.

At the time, Danilo's focus had been elsewhere. If anything the time he had spent learning his new role had actually felt more like relaxation, a form of escapism, something he could actually control while the thing that really mattered to him, his sister, he had no control over. All he could do was sit beside her hospital bed and now it seemed as though she didn't even want him there. The memories of a few days earlier were still fresh in his mind. His feelings of rejection were confusingly mangled with pride.

Nat had come to him the next morning and the first words out of her mouth were, 'I wasn't punishing you!'

Which made him pretty sure that she was. Nothing she said made it any clearer what he'd done but he reasoned he probably deserved punishment, if not for the mysterious sin he had committed recently, then for the very real and unforgivable piece of selfishness that had put her in the chair.

She had gone on to relay pretty much word for word what the doctor had said. There were no surprises and Nat seemed to have asked all the right questions. When he'd commented on it she'd smiled.

'I had a good teacher.'

He nodded pleasantly to one of the young grooms who looked surprised when he saw Danilo. His father would have remembered the man's name, he realised, thinking that despite the fact the financial world, which had waited for him to fail, had now decided he had filled his father's shoes more than adequately, Danilo knew better.

The moment he walked into the covered arena he saw her. The sight of her standing there dissolved the last shreds of any self-deception, leaving shock ricocheting around uncomfortably in his head.

He hadn't accidentally ended up in the place he knew Tess would be. *Fine, accepted...now move on.* He could have wasted hours trying to analyse a feeling that he couldn't put a name to, he could have let himself believe this woman had touched something inside him that no woman ever had, but that would have been an indulgence because there was no mystery involved. This was obviously about sex, or a lack of it; this was about the iron self-control he brought into play in his personal life failing him; this was about her being the most sensual, provocative creature he had ever encountered.

He wasn't happy about this situation, but pretending it didn't exist or making her feel uncomfortable to be in the same room as him provided no sort of solution, any more than applying a sticking plaster to a severed artery would prevent a victim bleeding out.

The question was what would?

There was a simple solution: he'd brought her here, an action he now privately likened to inviting an unexploded bomb into his home… his life, so he could send her away.

So obvious, so why wasn't he doing it?

Because this was about Nat, not him. Since Tess's arrival the change in his sister had been borderline miraculous. She had rediscovered some of her enthusiasm for life. The situation was still a work in progress and obviously there had been the London blip, there were still resentful silences and looks directed his way, but they were less and less frequent. Tess Jones might be making his life uncomfortable but her influence on Nat was all positive.

And it wasn't just Nat, and Franco, who acted like an attention-seeking puppy in her presence, but even his aunt, not a woman easily impressed, had referred to his sister's companion as a breath of fresh air, and a very sensible woman.

Jaw clenched, he ground his even white teeth over his mounting seething frustration, ashamed that he had ever considered snuffing out his sister's smile simply because he was frustrated.

The arena was dark after the sun outside and it took his eyes a few moments to adjust and for him to realise that there was a horse and rider in the far end of the area. He barely spared them a glance as he continued to stare at Tess. She was a spectator, watching not in the tiers of seats at the far end, but standing balanced in a pair of crazy spiky ankle boots on the bottom rung of the fence that surrounded the exercise area, her elbows resting on the top bar. Her chin was cushioned on top of her hands.

Her hair was drawn back smoothly from her face, secured at the nape of her neck by a thin leather thong. It fell in soft silky waves almost to her waist.

The pattern on her shirt was strident, bold swirls of clashing red and orange tucked into a pair of snug-fitting jeans, her tiny waist emphasised by the wide leather belt. Oblivious to his presence, she lifted both hands to wave at the distant figure on the horse, letting out a husky laugh and clutching wildly when she almost fell from her perch.

Dragging his gaze off her bottom, Danilo closed his eyes and exhaled a slow measured hiss of breath through flared nostrils. *Self-control! Dio*, it was going to require a miracle to douse the fire she lit in him!

The impulse to pull her off the rail and into him quelled even though the arousing image of his hands curving over her breasts remained. He opened his eyes. Three more weeks of this, or bend his self-imposed rule of keeping his sex life away from his family?

Weren't rules meant to be broken?

The step he took towards her was involuntary; where it would have taken him he'd never know because at that moment there was a sound of laughter. He automatically turned his head towards it and froze.

'What the hell is going on here?'

The sound of his furious voice drew a shocked gasp from Tess. For once the inner radar that seemed to alert her to his presence had failed her. She stepped back awkwardly from the rail.

'Hello.' It sounded stupid—not that he seemed to hear her; he was striding towards the closed gate of the manège, his intention clear. Knowing she had to stop him, she raced to his side, for once forgetting her no-touch policy as she grabbed his arm.

'Please don't go and drag her off. She'll be so embarrassed and she's having such a good time.'

'My sister is on a horse.' Tearing his eyes from the figure just long enough to direct a killer look at Tess's face, he ground out, 'My *paralysed* sister is on a horse.' It was the most terrifying thing he had ever witnessed. Sweat broke out as he watched. She looked small and the ground looked so far away.

'Yes, and she's having a great time.' Tess's attempt to lighten the mood fell flat.

She watched as he visibly paled with anger

then exploded, pinning her with a wrathful glare.

'This is all your doing. Without your influence Nat would not have dreamt of doing this.'

'Calm down.'

A few minutes earlier he had been telling himself she was good for his sister. The dark irony was not lost on him, though her appeal to *calm down* was.

'Calm down? My sister is riding!'

'You can thank me later.' *Too flippant, Tess*, she thought with an inner groan.

'*Dio!* I can understand that you get a kick out of thwarting me, I can tolerate that while you appear to make my sister happy, but you have put her in danger! You can pack your bags and stay the night in a hotel. I'll book a flight for you for tomorrow.'

Shock froze her to the spot, the colour seeping from her face as she stared up at him. 'You're *sacking* me?'

He raised a sardonic brow and turned away, his long fingers slipping the latch that led to the arena.

'But…but…' She tightened her grip on his forearm. Her stomach reacted to the contact as though she had just stepped off a tall building, but she didn't let the sensation distract her. This was too important.

'Please, Danilo!' she begged urgently.

His lips were curled in a silent snarl as he swung back.

'You can sack me if you like—'

'Good of you to give permission,' he sneered sarcastically.

'But please don't do this. It's a massive mistake and you'll regret it. It took a lot of courage for Nat to get on that horse and if you go over there now and embarrass her, Nat will—'

'Better embarrassed than injured.'

'She won't be—'

'How dare—?'

'I asked you. I asked and you said I could—I know it was a bit retrospective, I should have checked yesterday, but—'

'Make use of the stables, take out a horse—*you*, not my sister.' He stopped. 'Yesterday! This isn't the first time?'

She fought the instinct to retreat from the arctic blast of his furious glare and brought her lashes down in a concealing curtain. 'You didn't stop long enough for me to explain,' she muttered, the resentment that she recognised as irrational slipping past her guard. Since London there had been several occasions when they were alone when he had cut off a conversation abruptly, acting as though he couldn't get out of the room fast enough. The only reason she cared, she told herself, was that she hated bad manners.

'You knew what I thought and you could have put me right but you didn't because you knew that I would put a stop to this.'

'*This,* as you put it, is your sister having a good time, and I didn't tell you because Nat asked me *not* to. She wanted to surprise you.' And she hadn't wanted her brother to see her fail. 'And yes, I did encourage her, but I would never endanger Nat. She is totally safe. I used to help out at a stable that specialised in riding for the disabled, and there were people there with a lot worse disabilities than your sister.'

'My sister is not disabled. She is going to walk again!'

The fingers curled around his arm tightened as the amber eyes lifted to his warmed with sympathy… *Dio,* he had sacked her and she was feeling sorry for him.

'But until then don't you think it would be good for her to enjoy the things she can still do? Look at her face, Danilo—sack me if you like but don't spoil it for her,' she begged anxiously.

He flashed a look at the distant figure, took in the figures beside her and took a deep breath. 'If she falls—' he gritted through clenched teeth.

'They are walking,' Tess pointed out as at the same sedate pace the horse carrying Natalia began to move across the manège towards them. 'The horse is a pony. It has beautiful manners and she is being led.'

Danilo gave a grudging nod of stiff assent as the two grooms who walked either side of the pony brought the animal to a halt. The groom holding the leading rein moved closer to speak to his sister, her words indistinct at this distance.

'But the fact is even if it is a donkey you had no right to do this without discussing it with me.'

'I'm sorry.'

He gave a grunt. 'No, you're not.'

Tess shrugged and took advantage of the fact he seemed to be calming down. 'True, but there really is zero risk.' She pointed at the two girls walking alongside the horse and the third holding the leading rein. 'Please don't glower like that. It took a lot for Nat to get up there and in the end it was making you proud that swung it.'

'I am proud of her. I always am.'

'Then show it and smile.'

The admonishment drew a grunt of shock from Danilo. *Though God knows why*, he thought grimly. The woman could not open her mouth without telling him what he was doing wrong. What he needed was some time with a woman who appreciated him, not this witch with her talent for interfering and the innate conviction she knew what was good for everyone—or was that just him?

'I'm beginning to wonder how I survived before you arrived to tell me how to behave.'

'Oh, I expect you'll cope when I'm gone.'

He turned his head sharply. *'Gone!'*

'You sacked me.' A first, but it was not the humiliation of being sacked that bothered her, but the panic that had surged through her at the thought.

Panic that would have been understandable if it had been the fear of her stalker waiting for her at home that had caused it, but it wasn't. It was the idea of leaving, of never seeing Nat and...who was she kidding? The thing that had pressed her panic button was not seeing Danilo again.

A muscle in his lean cheek clenched as their eyes connected, the emotions swirling around them suddenly solidified into a tension that made it an effort for Tess to breathe.

'You make me—' The words seemed drawn out against his will and the effort of cutting them off showed in the tension in his face as he found relief in an explosive expletive.

'Angry, I know.' Her voice, breathy and strange, sounded as though it was coming from a long way off.

'You know that's not what I'm talking about.'

She shook her head, her courage for once deserting her. 'No—' Her denial was silenced by the brush of his thumb against her lips.

She stepped away from the contact with a gasp. 'What are you doing?'

Good question, Danilo, what are you doing?

His cobalt-blue stare had a hypnotic quality. Tess was suddenly fighting for breath as everything seemed to move into slow motion, everything but her heart that continued to batter against her ribcage.

'Danilo!'

The musical sound of his sister's happy voice made them both start. Tess pulled back first, her pale face flaming red, and, after staring at her for a moment longer, Danilo turned after, arranging his features in the requested smile. Behind him Tess began to clap. He could almost feel her relief when he joined in.

The beam of pride on his sister's face as she continued to approach at a snail's pace was worth gritting his teeth for.

Natalia laughed again. 'I'll get better. It was only my second time, but I can still do it, Danilo. I can still ride!'

For a split second before he responded his guard was fully down and Danilo looked almost vulnerable. The stark contrast between the pain and pride etched in the proud lines of his face sent a piercing stab of empathy she didn't want to feel through Tess, who stood silently watching.

Removing the hand she had instinctively reached out to cover a white-knuckled fist that hung at his side—the gesture, she knew, would not be appreciated—she pressed it instead to her throat where an emotional lump ached. Blinking hard, she turned her head sharply away, taking a moment to regain control before she trusted herself to speak.

'So I see.'

'We dismount over there. Wait here.'

He took an involuntary step forwards as the horse turned. Tess caught his arm.

'Let her, Danilo, don't spoil it,' she begged huskily.

'Is that what you think I do?' He tore his eyes from the smile on his sister's face, turning his attention to the heart-shaped face looking up at him. '*Spoil* things?' He felt as if he were walking around with a weight attached to his chest, but he knew naming his emotions would not make it easier. He didn't deserve easier.

'Smile, please. And don't blame Nat. This is my doing, so if you're going to be mad with anyone—'

'I never doubted who was to blame,' he ground out between clenched teeth as his sister, who was several yards away now on her stationary mount, yelled over.

'Don't watch me, Danilo, we have this covered. I don't need your help. You make me nervous. Wait over there—both of you.'

'You heard her, come on.'

Danilo had heard her and he'd heard the imperious tone he had almost forgotten about as he tipped his head in acknowledgement of the order, and with a glimmer of a smile he called out to her, '*Sì*, Principessa.'

With a tight hold on the pommel, Nat, and the horse responding to the urging of a groom, turned to face them. 'You haven't called me that for ages.'

'You haven't been bossy for ages,' he tossed back.

'It's quite nice looking down on you for a change.'

It only took him a couple of long-legged strides to catch up with Tess, who was walking towards the tier of seats that Natalia had banished them to. 'I suppose you want me to say you were right and I was wrong?'

'This isn't about being right, or being wrong, though you are. Actually I have no problem with you not being infallible, but you clearly do.' Beside her Danilo stopped and she carried on walking, missing the expression on his face.

A moment later he caught her up and fell into step beside her.

'I used to come here and watch our mother in the ring.'

'Nat said she was very good.'

He nodded. 'She gave up an international career in show-jumping and a place on the national equestrian team when she married.' They had reached the tier of spectator seats but Danilo didn't sit down; instead he turned and stared out at the empty ring.

'My mum says a woman doesn't have to give up anything. She didn't.'

'Everyone is different. Seeing our mother on a horse…it was special, but it was her choice.' Even though it had never seemed right to Danilo.

'I've always been scared of horses. They're unpredictable.' A bit like Danilo, she thought, as she took the end seat in the bottom row.

'Nat used to love riding. Seeing her there just now has made me realise that she is growing up to be very like our mother and not just in looks. I saw my mother fall once when I was a kid. She looked so white lying there.' He nodded to the ring. 'I thought she was dead. They airlifted her to hospital. The next day she was back in the saddle with a fractured collarbone strapped up.' He stopped. 'You're scared of horses?' And he had spent the morning imagining her on horseback.

'No, just of heights.'

He laughed. 'But you helped at a stable?'

'My feet firmly on the ground. Mum encouraged me to get involved with community projects. I didn't always enjoy them but the stables were different. It was really rewarding to see how much confidence people gained. Being on horseback is a great leveller.'

Natalia did look happy. He felt a slug of guilt. This was the way she should have looked every day if he had been there for her. The way she would look when she walked again.

'So are you all right with this? She can carry on with the lessons? I'm forgiven?'

The soft question brought his dark gaze zeroing in on Tess's face as he acknowledged that there was nothing to forgive her for. That moment of gut-wrenching fear he had experienced when he'd seen Nat on the horse had made him lash out at Tess. 'She can carry on with the lessons,' he said, struggling to detach himself from the heavy weight of guilt in his chest.

The omission might not have been significant but the stab of hurt Tess felt was!

She pushed away the recognition as Natalia brought her chair to a halt beside her brother.

CHAPTER EIGHT

'I DIDN'T BELIEVE I could do it, but Tess said.'
She flashed silent Tess a beaming smile. 'She
said I could.'

Danilo looked at Natalia's glowing face and
found himself wishing that he'd been the one
to put the happy shine in her eyes.

'So what do you think?'

Tess was worried to find she could identify
so strongly with the need for approval that
shone in the younger girl's eyes.

'You weren't meant to see me until I'd got
better.'

'You were tremendous!'

She smiled happily and agreed. 'Yes, I was,
wasn't I?' She performed an acrobatic one-
hundred-and-eighty-degree turn in her chair
that made Danilo wince, though he did man-
age to bite back a cautionary admonition to
take care—*just*.

'Where are you off to now, conquering

Everest?' He had no doubt that if Tess suggested it Nat would have a go.

'No, that's next week. I have physio and…' she glanced down at her watch '…I'm late. Come on, Tess.'

'Can I borrow Tess for a moment?'

'Sure, but what do you want with her?'

A veiled look slid into Danilo's eyes, though it was the heightened colour along his cheekbones that caught Tess's attention—on anyone else she would have called it a blush. But when he spoke he sounded casual enough. 'Your birthday is coming up and you should not ask too many questions.'

At this reminder the slight furrow that remained in her brow faded. Danilo was happy to see the sparkle rekindled in her eyes but less happy at the voice in his head that reminded him it was there *despite* him and because of Tess.

'Fine,' Nat tossed over her shoulder before she paused, reminding Tess, 'But remember, we need to be at the hairdresser's for three thirty.'

Danilo stiffened as the words killed off any softening of his attitude.

'Oh, we've bags of time,' Tess called back before the girl sped off in her chair.

Danilo waited for his sister to be out of earshot before he turned to Tess, saying flatly, 'Cancel!'

He watched her smile gutter as she blinked up at him in apparent bemusement, so he spelt it out. 'The hairdresser comes here.'

It was impossible to tell from her expression just how much his autocratic delivery had aggravated her. 'Half the fun of having your hair done is hearing the gossip and watching other people. You wouldn't understand. It's called being sociable.'

He refused to play her game and rise to the bait. He was not going to allow his little sister to endure the ordeal her last trip out had involved.

'You couldn't know,' he admitted, trying to be fair. Which was the only thing at that moment stopping him coming down on her really hard. 'But the last time Natalia went to a beauty salon there was an…incident—'

Tess nodded. 'When the bathroom doors at the place were not wide enough to accommodate her wheelchair?'

'She told you?' When he had raised the subject later his sister had said she never wanted to talk about it.

Tess nodded.

'And yet you…' He shook his head in an attitude of disbelief, recalling the mortified tears running down Nat's cheeks when she had relayed the incident. 'Unbelievable! If you had a shred of imagination or half the empathy you like to pretend…' Words seemed to fail him. 'You know what I think?' he gritted out.

Tess was fed up making excuses for his autocratic attitude, making allowances for *his* feelings. She shrugged, reminding herself that she *didn't* care what Danilo thought of her. 'Wild guess…you're going to tell me?'

'I don't think you give a damn about Nat. The only thing you care about is being proved right. You just have to meddle! Well, I suggest you get your own life in order before you start interfering in others'.' She flinched, and for a moment he almost wished the words unsaid—*almost*.

'Let me spell out the situation. *They* come to *her*.' Nat had picked out her season's wardrobe from the comfort of home, she had beauticians, hairdressers and the like on speed dial, and she was not to be fobbed off with a trainee.

'It's a trip to the hairdresser's,' Tess said in a small but determined voice. She didn't want to make an issue of this but she would.

He breathed out, the air hissing through his clenched teeth. 'You would expose Nat to insult just to prove some point?'

'What point?' she echoed, bewildered. 'I'm not trying to prove any point.'

'You walk in here and…you can't keep your nose out of anything, can you?'

Tess's head came up with a jerk. 'This isn't about me.'

'Everything is about you, since you arrived.' He dragged a frustrated hand through his hair and glared down at her glossy head.

'I don't like to see people unhappy, and if I can—'

'Bring a little light into their lives? Well, I don't need a damn sunbeam.'

What do you need, Danilo?

Her head spun. He had covered the space between them in a couple of strides and stood there towering over her, but when he spoke his voice was soft and every syllable carried a warning that made her shiver. 'And for the record, *I* am not a nice person.'

She heard the warning in each soft syllable but stood her ground, not because she was brave or stupid, but because her feet felt as though they were literally nailed to the ground. Being this close to him felt like standing on the brink of a live volcano. Close enough to feel the heat of his body as he towered over her, Tess could feel the waves of frustrated anger rolling off him.

'You think that I would not do *anything* for my sister!' he rasped out.

'I think you'd do anything for your sister, including keeping her hidden away in her golden cage, never leaving in case someone looks at her the wrong way.'

The coiled tension in his bunched muscles didn't lessen, but as she watched the dull colour run up under his olive-toned skin she felt a stab of sympathy push through her own hurt and anger. She worried at the plump, soft flesh of her lower lip with her teeth. Hell, it ought to be easy to dislike him but it wasn't. Danilo was devoted to his sister and that was the problem. He wanted to protect Nat from everything, and the poor girl, who worshipped him, let him.

'That is a gross exaggeration,' he managed finally.

She responded with a shrug. 'If you say so.'

'I do,' Danilo gritted through clenched teeth.

'You can't protect her from everything,' Tess said quietly. 'Obviously *that* salon won't be getting her custom but you underestimate her, you know. She is a fighter. She realises that the thing to do if people are ignorant is not to hide away but to educate them.'

The fact that what Tess said made sense only increased Danilo's levels of seething frustration and resentment towards her. 'And is this little lesson intended for me?'

She gave a rueful grimace and accompanied her response with an eloquent shrug of her slender shoulders. 'Sorry, you can take a teacher out of the classroom but—'

Jaw clenched, he ignored the olive-branch apology. 'I am not one of your little five-year-olds, Miss Jones, and I am not impressed by homespun fortune-cookie philosophy.'

'Then it's just as well I'm not interested in impressing you,' she snapped back, losing what sympathy she felt in the face of his refusal to relinquish his control over his sister—talk about tunnel vision!

Talking to this man was like banging her head against a stone wall. 'I realise,' she continued with acid sweetness, 'it probably makes you feel big and strong to rush to the rescue of helpless maidens, but we're not *all* weak and helpless. Some of us, the ones who don't feel it necessary to consult the great Danilo Raphael before we decide what side of the bed to get out of in the morning, can actually look after ourselves!' she finished, breathless and struggling to hold on to her attitude of self-righteous scorn—he looked mad again, *extremely* mad!

Halfway in she had been regretting her impetuous words, born of sheer frustration, but they had just kept coming and now, as she stood there hands on hips refusing to give him the satisfaction of seeing her take refuge behind one of the large bales of hay, she was *really* wishing that she had kept to the safe moral high ground instead of sinking to his level.

Danilo allowed his eyelids to flicker downwards, giving himself time to recover from the scene that was playing inside his head. The mental image involved Tess getting out of bed naked. It was a distraction that even his strong mental control was unable to banish, but he was able to use the same control to think past it and ignore the physical responses that he had zero control over.

It was crazy. Tess was attractive, sure, but in no way his *type*. This was what happened to a man when he ignored basic needs: they came back to bite him! He should have spent the night with Alex even if that had meant closing his eyes and thinking of...

Of their own volition his eyes slid to Tess's mouth. Did she bi…? He stopped the thought. There were some things about Miss Jones he *didn't* need to know.

Who are you kidding, Danilo?

He forcibly dragged his gaze from her mouth and told himself the sooner the better that he did something about the desert his sex life had been of late. If not Alex, there were others who did not contradict him at every turn. It was a matter of carving some time into his hectic schedule or going quietly insane; he needed meaningless sex urgently. At the moment, he could not afford any other sort— not that the situation was proving a hardship for him.

In the past he'd had what could be loosely termed long-term—as in three or four months—relationships, and he knew they required more time and energy than he was prepared at the moment to devote to his sex life. And those sorts of relationships had a habit of spilling over into the other parts of his life, and he appreciated how much more smoothly life ran when you compartmentalised. Sex was necessary as food was necessary, but not while there were more important things to deal with, like filling his father's shoes, and seeing his sister walk. He had no space left for the inevitable emotional demands of a relationship when it moved on from being simple sex.

'I do not need women to be weak to feel like a man, and you were not coping so well alone.' He watched her pale at the below-the-belt hit and immediately felt like a total heel.

'Well, I walked into that one, didn't I?' She gave a crooked smile, a characteristic he had come to recognise was very much her own, and she spread her arms wide, causing the sleeveless blouse she was wearing to ride up and reveal a sliver of tummy.

Half an inch and it sent a flash of heat through Danilo's already overheated body. He reacted with anger.

'You never walk. You jump, you run, you'd throw yourself off a cliff if it felt like the right thing to do. And while you do the right thing the rest of us... Do you know what *I* felt like when I saw Nat sitting on the back of that damned horse?' He dragged a hand across the stubble that had erupted on his jaw since he had shaved that morning and watched her eyes soften with compassion. She just didn't seem to get that he was not a man who needed compassion, or sympathy, or anything else from her.

Nothing, Danilo?

He ignored the inner voice but couldn't stop the hungry journey of his eyes as they slid down her body and made the return trip a lot slower.

'I can see that. I know I should probably have run it by you.'

One dark brow lifted. 'You think?'

'But you heard Nat. She wanted to surprise you.'

'Job well done,' he said grimly.

'I thought you were all right with it now?'

'I am. It's you I'm not all right with!' he bellowed then without warning. 'I'm beginning to dread coming home.' It wasn't until he made the claim that Danilo realised that the opposite was true. 'You realise the position you've put me in, don't you? If I forbid Natalia to do it again I'm the monster. You like to turn me into a monster, don't you?'

She rolled her eyes, exasperated by his determination to misrepresent everything she said. 'I don't think you're a monster. I think you're—' His upheld hand stopped her.

'Don't tell me, please. I doubt my ego would survive.'

She arched a sceptical brow but her laugh was strained. His lofty attitude of amused indifference made her want to stamp her foot but that really would have given him something to laugh at.

'I think your ego is armour plated.' She had never encountered anyone with arrogance and a sense of superiority so bred into the bone. *Beautiful bones.* She brought her lashes down in a concealing sweep, ignored the twisting sensation and counted silently to ten before lifting her gaze to the man towering over her.

'You can't wrap your sister up in cotton wool. Well, you can, because I suppose you can do pretty much what you like, and it's true she'll be safe, but what sort of life will that be for her, Danilo?'

The appeal in her eyes passed Danilo by. He was unable to think past her assumption that he was free to act on impulses. His eyes darkened as his gaze slid to her mouth. If that were true…

'You think I can do what I like?' Had she made the accusation a few years ago she'd have been right. Back then he'd done what he liked, he'd lived for the moment. His idea of responsibility had been remembering his mother's birthday and having Christmas dinner at home. Now he couldn't remember the last time he'd acted on impulse.

And then he remembered: he'd brought Tess Jones into their lives. His eyes slid to the up-turned face of the woman standing there, hands on her slender hips, smiling that infuriating, damned condescending smile of hers. Hell, he'd spent a morning closeted with a bunch of powerful individuals who had treated him with respect and sought his approval and he'd come home to this little slip of a woman who showed him not a jot of respect and had demonstrated on every occasion possible she didn't give a damn about pleasing him.

'Well, I don't see anyone telling *you* what to do,' she replied.

'Except you! You go out of your way to disagree with me, challenge my authority.'

'Maybe,' she countered, 'I don't recognise your authority. People say what they think you want to hear because they're scared of you!' she threw back.

He flinched, the white line etched around his sensual lips growing more defined as he lost the last remnants of his air of amused indifference. 'Are you suggesting my sister is scared of me?' he demanded, outraged by the suggestion.

'Not in that way. She just likes to please you. Just because you're a benevolent tyrant, it doesn't mean you're not a tyrant. It wouldn't do you any harm once in a while to listen rather than dictate.'

'Any more words of wisdom you care to bestow?'

Well, why not? Tess thought. If she was going to be shown the door there was no point biting her tongue. She might as well get it all off her chest.

'You're not *always* right, Danilo, and you know it—'

'The only thing I know is—' There was a strong element of compulsion in his expression and his action as he raised his hand and touched her cheek.

Totally unprepared for his touch, Tess startled, like one of the highly strung thoroughbreds in the stables, and took a hasty step back. She stood there, her breath coming in a series of tiny uneven pants, her shimmering golden stare trained on his face as she slowly lifted her hand to her cheek. Her skin still tingled from the brief contact and her stomach was quivering violently.

'Wh-why…did you do that?'

'I didn't *want* to.' He shook his head, unwilling to admit even to himself that the *need* that had flared without warning inside him was stronger than sense or reason. His nostrils flared as his burning gaze remained trained on her face.

What he wasn't saying, what was glowing in his incredible eyes, excited Tess in a way she had never experienced before. She watched as he lifted a hand and dragged it across his hair, making the black strands stand up in sexy spikes.

'Ever since you arrived here—'

He stopped abruptly, as if he could not force the words past the thickening atmosphere that quivered with tension. It reminded her of that stillness before a storm.

Always overpoweringly conscious of his physical presence, his raw masculinity, she felt that awareness jump, reaching an almost cellular level.

Tess's pulses did some leaping of their own as she struggled to drag her eyes from the muscle that was clenching and unclenching in his cheek.

His voice was so deep it was barely more than a whisper. The driven expression made her want to run away, but for some reason by the time the message reached her brain it said something different. Her eyes didn't leave his face as she took a step towards him. As she moved closer his hands closed over her upper arms and he impatiently dragged her into him until their bodies were close enough for her to feel the heat of his body, feel the tension in his muscles, inhale the scent of his skin.

It was an unimaginable situation and yet she had pictured it; the knowledge came with a rush of head-spinning excitement. Somewhere in the back of her mind there lingered a small corner, a fragment of sanity that was telling her this was a bad idea, but she determinedly ignored it.

'Say my name.'

She swallowed, the emotions swirling inside her making her throat close.

'I want to hear you say it.'

Her head dropped but even with her eyes squeezed tight shut she could still see his eyes, the burn in the midnight depths that awoke a need in her she had never experienced.

His hand went under her chin. Tess resisted, not the strong fingers drawing her face to him, but the heavy drag of desire low in her belly, the heat that made her shiver and her oversensitised skin tingle. Even as she fought she recognised the futility of the attempt. What was happening, and she had no name for it, was happening at a primal level.

Her head tilted back, her neck suddenly not strong enough to support her but it didn't need to, because his hand had moved, his fingers providing a supportive cradle at the back of her head. Her heart was drumming so hard with anticipation that it drowned out her husky whisper.

'Danilo.'

He sighed and smiled a slow smile, made up of equal parts predatory intent and heart-stopping tenderness. The combination killed off any lingering resistance as lust, hot and hungry, cut through the dreamy desire.

As he bent his head she reached up her hands, linking them behind his neck. The slowness felt like torture as he bent his head until his mouth was a bare half-inch from hers. She could feel the warm waft of his breath on her skin before he brushed his lips over the corners of her mouth, and, holding her gaze, he ran his tongue along the quivering outline.

Tess whimpered, the sound lost inside the warmth of his mouth as it finally captured her own. As the slow, sensuous possession deepened it lost finesse and became rough, hungry and raw. The feelings tearing through her were like nothing she had ever experienced or imagined.

She was not conscious of walking backwards until her back made contact with the stone wall of the building. Still kissing her, he slid his hands down her body, one moving to cup the curve of her bottom. She instinctively arched her back, pushing into him, only pulling back slightly as she felt the imprint of his arousal against the softness of her belly.

He said something, she didn't know what, and she wound her arms around his neck, letting her head fall back as he trailed hot, damp kisses down her throat.

If anyone saw us now they'd assume we were making... She sucked in a startled breath. And they'd be right, or at least they would be if this didn't stop now.

Right now, Tess!

Digging deep into her reserves, she placed her hands flat on his chest and pushed back. After a moment he reacted to the pressure and let her go. Her knees felt so weak that if it hadn't been for the stone wall behind her she'd have slid to the floor.

'You're right. Not here, not now,' Danilo said, thinking more clearly than he had done in days. He could see now that he'd been looking at this problem from the wrong angle. Trying to keep Tess at arm's length was like trying to put out a forest fire with a watering can.

Lighting more fires seemed counter-intuitive but giving that initial conflagration no place to go was an acknowledged method to quench a wild fire. Let it burn itself out but keep it within boundaries.

This was the point where Tess knew she was meant to say, *not anywhere, not ever*, but she didn't. As she stared up at him all the feelings he aroused in her narrowed into one beam of white-hot desire that blasted away the image of a face that had haunted her for half her life. The sense of liberation made her feel light-headed.

Acknowledging that the ugly incident from her past had not gone away but spread out ugly roots from the dark corner she had consigned it to had been half of the healing process. Losing her virginity would complete it.

She wanted to have sex with the most gorgeous man on the planet and if he ended up breaking her heart she would deal with that later. In the meantime she was going to enjoy it, and so what if all he wanted was her body? She could deal with it.

'Only don't carry on looking at me with those big hungry eyes or I'll…' He took a deep breath and dragged a hand across his hair, somehow managing to look totally normal seconds later, when he tipped his head her way as though they had just exchanged nothing more intimate than a good morning while she was shaking inside and out.

If that was good morning, imagine goodnight!

CHAPTER NINE

'WELL, WHAT DO you think?'

Tess blinked. 'Think?'

'You haven't heard a thing I've said, have you?' Natalia angled a speculative look at Tess's face. 'And you keep smiling.'

'Do I?'

'Is it that guy at the coffee bar? I saw him give you his number. He was hot!'

Tess, who had forgotten the crumpled piece of paper in her pocket, smiled and tried to look mysterious. 'Maybe.' She could hardly say, *I was thinking about your brother kissing me.* She frowned as she thought of Danilo walking away. *Not here, not now.*

She really wished she had asked for more details. That she'd pinned him down to a time and a place. Astonished at the way she was thinking, she took a deep breath and looked at Natalia, who was happily chatting away.

She didn't have a clue what she'd been talking about; all she'd been fantasising about was being made love to by Danilo.

By that evening, it looked as if the fantasy was going to remain just that. Danilo was not at the *palazzo* when they returned and he was a no show at dinner. The meal was a nightmare! Tess smiled through gritted teeth listening to Franco's jokes about his cousin's workload being blonde and six feet in heels, then refused the suggestion of a film session. She really wasn't in the mood for watching a cool blonde Hitchcock heroine ensnare her man.

She felt like a total and complete idiot. She'd finally decided to give herself to a man and he'd lost interest, or had a better offer. Who knew…who cared?

Me, she thought miserably as she tipped half a flagon of bath oil into the copper tub that took centre stage in her massive en-suite bathroom.

The bath was running when she heard a knock on the door and she called out, 'Hold on!' as she paused to switch off the taps. A leak in the ceiling of the *palazzo* could destroy a priceless fresco.

She opened the door, expecting to see one

of the maids who turned down her bed each night, and instead saw Danilo standing there looking cool. But that illusion vanished as soon as she met his eyes. The dark slow burn she saw there lit a fuse inside her in the time it took for her heart to take a lurching thud, all her earlier anger fading.

It was mad, it was crazy, it was utterly illogical but she wanted to be with him tonight, actually any night.

Without a word he stretched his hand towards her.

Tess looked at his long brown tapering fingers and imagined them on her skin. A second later she laid her hand in his.

She jogged to keep up with his pace.

'Where are we going?'

'Somewhere we can be private. This is it, my room.' He walked ahead of her, through the door, and stood to one side as she entered.

Danilo's private apartment was in the north-facing wing of the *palazzo*. She'd never been here before though she'd often wondered what it was like, but as he closed the door behind her Tess felt no urge to study the decor.

Danilo was a work of art, she decided, making a covert study of him. The angle of his head, the strong line of his back, the strong musculature and power of his thighs hinted at by the well-cut linen trousers he wore.

The click of the key as he turned it in the lock broke her rapt concentration.

It's really happening, then, she thought as he turned to face her.

She didn't realise his intention when he caught her hand, turned it over until it was palm up and unfolded her fingers one by one to expose her palm.

She stared at the key he placed in it before he closed her fingers and his hand over it.

'To keep them out, not you in. You can walk through that door any time you want to, you know that?'

She swallowed, struggling to force the words past the aching occlusion in her throat, but there was no hesitation before she handed the key back to him.

'I don't need it. There's nowhere else I want to be right now.'

And right now was all that mattered, she told herself and waited for the flurry of panic to subside. It did. The now was all that mattered, all that she could *allow* to matter, and she refused to think beyond it, beyond to a future that didn't contain Danilo.

'You're sure?'

His voice had sounded not quite steady. By comparison, her response was. 'Totally.'

With a nod, he inhaled through flared nostrils. She watched as he slid the key back into the lock and turned back to face her, his dark eyes seeking out and fastening onto her exotic, wide-spaced amber eyes. The unvarnished carnality of his stare sent a deep shudder through her receptive body. Tess snatched in air through parted lips when, without breaking contact, he began to unbutton his shirt.

Tess swallowed, breathing hard, her eyelids fluttering as she fought the compulsion to watch. She lasted until he slipped the last button and then she couldn't *not* look.

A deep, tremulous sigh escaped her parted lips.

The shirt hung open to the waist revealing a section of his flat, muscle-ridged belly and the light dusting of body hair on his broad, powerful chest that narrowed into a directional arrow as it vanished under the belt that hung low on his narrow hips.

The image imprinted itself on her retina as her skin heated. She moistened her lips and thought about touching him, thought about unfastening the silver buckle and...her thoughts shocked and excited her.

'Now your turn.'

It took a few moments for her lust-soaked brain to work out what he had said, what he was asking her to do. Her eyes widened and from some primal corner of her mind the confidence to do what he asked, not just because he asked but because she *wanted* to, came.

Shoulders back, she lifted her chin, her stance challenging him as she walked slowly towards him. She didn't stop until she was close enough to feel the heat coming from his body.

His eyes were hot too, hot enough to singe her as she held them for a moment before she turned around presenting her slender back to him. She could hear the sound of his harsh, rapid breathing above the thud of her heartbeat as she gathered the long skein of her hair in one hand and lifted it off her neck in silent invitation.

Her breath came quick and shallow as he slowly pulled down the zip of the silk shift dress she was wearing. The light contact of his fingertips on the damp skin of her back sent little shivers of sensation across her skin as they moved downwards until her back and the dimple above the upper curve of her taut bottom were exposed.

She stood there for a moment, feeling his stare burning into her back, then, taking a deep breath, she retraced her steps until she reached the spot where she had begun and turned. Holding his eyes, she slid her loosened dress off one shoulder then the other.

Danilo watched, his eyes half shaded by his heavy lids and thick lashes leaving just a glittering slit visible. He was fighting for each breath like someone oxygen-deprived. Each laboured inhalation lifted his ribcage and pulled his flat belly concave, all the while his eyes remaining trained on her face.

It wasn't until she let the dress fall, jiggling her hips as it slipped in a silken slither to her ankles, that his glance dropped.

She heard his raw gasp of, *'Che Dio mi aiuti...'* as she stepped away from the silken pool at her feet, and, head tilted to one side, took a step towards him and stood there poised, reminding him of a deer not sure whether to run away or towards the light. She stood before him, an incredibly arousing combination of wantonness and innocence in her pose.

Perfect, he thought as he greedily absorbed every detail, every perfect inch of her as she stood there in her heels, tiny pants, a bra that consisted of little more than two triangles of silk, so fine he could see not just the outline of her prominent nipples through it but the darker shadow of the areola.

She was beautiful. More than beautiful. Skin that pale and perfect did not exist, he had thought, outside the airbrushed photo spreads in glossy magazines. But she represented everything that was female and desirable. He was unable to take his eyes off her, his restless gaze remaining riveted as he moved towards her.

Tess gave a tiny cry and ran, meeting him halfway.

The impact of their collision was softened when his arm, resembling a band of steel, wrapped around her waist before, almost casually, he lifted her off her feet and dragged her against him in one smooth, effortless motion.

The delicious shock of skin-to-skin contact vibrated along her nerve endings, and combined with the arousing power of his display of strength it made her head start to spin. She didn't even connect the low feral moan with her as she reached out greedily for him, her fingers digging into the thick glossy pelt of hair, pushing deeper and holding him there as he found her mouth.

The kiss, hard, hungry, seemed to go on for ever, or at least until the heat that unfurled in her belly had ribboned out throughout her entire body until she was aflame, her sensitised skin tingling, her insides liquid. The hunger his kiss had awoken was relentless, all consuming, something outside her experience or imagination.

As he continued the carnally creative kiss Tess twisted in his arms, her attempt to wrap her legs around him aided when he grunted and shifted her higher up without breaking contact.

When he finally lifted his head they were both breathing hard.

Her legs still secured around his waist, she held his face between her hands. 'I like that a lot,' she told him.

Her fierce declaration dragged a raw laugh from his throat as he stared into her passion-glazed eyes with a mixture of hunger and fascination. '*Madre di Dio, cara,* so do I. I have never met a woman like you.'

'You are perfect!'

'It will be perfect,' he promised thickly as he kissed her again. Tess's lips parted without pressure, inviting the carnal intrusion of his tongue and meeting it with her own.

They stumbled, bodies entwined, until Danilo's legs made contact with the bed. He turned as he looked down into her passion-flushed face, her golden eyes glowing, waiting… She was the living embodiment of temptation. His heartbeat slowed, leaving the impression that they were suspended in time.

The impression was fleeting; the moment passed but the pressure in his chest didn't. It grew; he felt he couldn't breathe. The unfamiliar feelings that broke loose inside him as he looked at her increased in intensity, stronger than anything he had ever experienced. A mingling of tenderness and passion, the combination was as contradictorily confusing as this woman was. As their eyes caught and held he felt a surge of possessiveness that drew a growl from his chest, as all the disparate feeling she evoked in him narrowed to one—passion! Hot and dark, like nothing he could remember feeling, it gripped him now as in his imagination. He felt her female warmth gripping him, holding him tight in a slick silken sheath.

Breathless, she blinked up at him, not sure how she came to be sitting on the edge of the bed, but she was. Danilo seemed a long way away looking down at her. She wanted him on top of her, inside her, not miles away, then as she opened her mouth to voice her complaint he dropped to his knees at her feet.

She stared at his dark head as he lifted first one, unhooking her shoe before he slid it off and flung it over his shoulder. Then he did the same to her right foot. A tiny shocked gasp left her lips as he raised her foot and ran a finger slowly along the delicate arch before lifting it to his lips and kissing it. She shuddered.

By the time he had applied the same methodology to her other foot she was shaking like someone with a fever, a heat that burned away the last shred of sanity she retained. There was nothing left but deep, drowning need.

'Please…'

A pulse throbbed in his temple, pounding with the effort it cost not to respond to the carnal, throaty plea.

Every instinct inside him screamed protest when, instead of pushing her down and falling on top of her the way they both wanted, he caught her hands and pulled her to her feet.

He couldn't stop his hands sliding down to her bottom, curling over the peachlike curves, drawing her into him until their bodies collided and he heard her gasp.

She was too weak with lust to hold her head

up; it fell back but not before, through heavy, half-closed eyes, she saw the taut, almost feral expression on Danilo's face. The image of it imprinted on her retina and she felt herself sinking deeper into the sexual thrall that held her tight in its grip.

Suddenly, she found herself sprawled onto the bed, her heart thudding as he lowered himself until, one knee braced on the mattress and a hand under her head, he loomed over her.

In mute supplication she held up her hands to him, her face a mask of need as she slid them over the sweet, slick miles of his powerful shoulder and back.

But instead of finally feeling the weight of his body on her, which was what she wanted, what she needed, the mattress lifted as he stood up until only their fingertips were touching.

He had not meant to let things go this far. He needed—it was important to say this, be upfront, not… His focus slipped, the urgency faded as he looked at her mouth and, unable to resist the temptation, the soft pink lushness offered, he bent his head.

The kiss that started at one corner of her

mouth was softer than the others and then it
wasn't. Her lips parted as his body, supported
on one elbow, leaned over her. As his tongue
slid inside her mouth she met it with her own,
the ache inside her now frantic and inarticu-
late, but Danilo was speaking. Half the things
he said were in his native tongue so she didn't
understand them, but it didn't seem to matter.
It was all wildly exciting, his eyes, his touch,
his mouth. They said the things that really
mattered.

He slid his hands down her bare shoulders
and pressed his lips to the hollow above her
collarbone.

Tess's head fell back as the kisses trailed in
the direction of the valley between her breasts
and he groaned. 'Your skin is so soft.'

Her hands glided over the muscles of his
back, each individually delineated. The beauty
of the perfect formation was not blurred by an
ounce of excess flesh. He was hard and lean.

'I can't believe this is happening. You're incredible.'

And then to her utter dismay he stepped
back, stood up and held up his hands as though
he was warding her off.

Confused, she sat up. 'Danilo…'

'No!'

Her expression as she crossed her hands across her chest, the hurt shining in her eyes, almost snapped his resolve. If she had been anyone else he would have said *to hell with it* right there and then.

'You need to know this is something I don't do.' He closed his eyes and huffed out a deep, long, steadying breath.

His face was taut with the effort it had cost him to pull back. The pain of it was etched deep into the lines of stress bracketing his mouth.

She would have been more hurt if it hadn't been for the driven need that glowed in his darkened eyes, the layer of moisture that glistened on his bronzed torso, and the fact that he was panting deep, gulping breaths, as though he'd just run a marathon.

That makes two of us, she thought, getting angry instead. 'Have sex?'

He ignored the comment. 'Bring my personal life into this house.'

'You mean sex life.' It amazed her that she could sound so calm.

He nodded. 'If this happens—'

If it didn't happen here and now whatever he was about to say wouldn't matter, couldn't matter, because she would die; she would die from sheer *wanting.* She would die a *virgin* of sheer wanting, which was even worse!

'It will not make us a couple. I have no time in my life at the moment to devote to a relationship.'

'But you have time for sex?'

'Tess, you are not making this...'

'Easy? It is easy. You don't have to agonise. I already know what you're working up towards—telling me that you don't want emotional entanglements, that you don't want your family, and I'm assuming anyone else, to know that we are sleeping together—if we ever actually get around to it. So, bottom line, it's a sort of "what happens behind closed doors stays there", which is fine by me. And outside the bedroom we carry on as normal, which shouldn't be too hard. I'll be leaving in three weeks, which is why I'm talking so fast.'

The last comment drew a sharp laugh from him.

She had mimed a ticking motion as she went through the list and now she threw the invisible list over her shoulder and rose to her feet, facing him, hands on hips.

'So far so good but in this same spirit of complete disclosure I need to tell you something. It might surprise you,' she warned.

It was Danilo who sat down on the bed this time. 'That will not be a first. You are not about to break the news that you started life as a man?'

'I'm a virgin.'

'No, joking aside.'

'Not a joke.'

The smile slipped from his face and was replaced by a guarded expression.

'Years ago something happened, well, it didn't, but it was scary and I think that every time I came near to…it got in the way—'

'What happened?'

'It doesn't matter. The important thing is I'm dealing with it now.'

'Yes, it does matter.'

She glanced at his face, took a deep breath and told him.

He sat and listened, not speaking, not moving until she had finished, his over-stillness at sharp variance with the emotions breaking loose inside him. Anger poured through him in a steady stream, mingled with outrage and a protective surge too strong to deny.

'So what did your mother do when you told her?'

'I didn't. There was no point—she would have felt so guilty and he never came back.'

'So who have you told?'

'Just you.'

Just you. The words echoed in his head.

'That's why I think that over the years it sort of grew into something more than it was.'

'It was what it was—an assault! Such men, I would…' He slid into his native tongue but Tess got the drift of his savage outpouring before, feelings vented, he held out a hand, ignoring the voice in his head that reminded him he'd wanted just sex and already it was more.

After the tiniest of pauses she laid her hand in his, only to pull back when he asked, 'Why now, and why me?'

She shrugged, not quite meeting his eyes. 'I don't know.' Or didn't want to know. 'Right time, the way we met? It was… You make me feel safe and at the same time…' She ran a tongue across her dry lips. 'I really like the way you make me feel and I think it helps that all you want from me is…well, sex, because—' She let out a light shriek as he reached out, grabbed her and pulled her on top of him.

As he rolled her beneath him, breathless, she arched up into him as, supporting himself on his elbows, he kissed his way up her body. 'Do you mind about, you know…?'

He had reached her chest and as he slid one

breast from the silken covering and fitted his mouth to the rosy peak she let out a low keening cry, half pain, half pleasure.

'It's a responsibility, but only a problem if we let it be,' he growled out as he lowered himself down onto her. 'I just want to make it as special for you as possible.'

She moaned and grabbed him, her fingers sliding down the slick skin of his back under the loosened shirt.

He levered himself up and began to fight his way out and then they were both tearing off clothes, their own and each other's, with frantic breathless urgency that did not make for speed but definitely raised the excitement stakes as they touched and kissed and tasted their way to freedom.

Tess was pretty much mindless with need by the time they were both fully naked. She wanted to explore every inch of him. He was so beautiful but she wanted so much more.

Then, as she was lying there naked, breathless, her entire body burning up with need, she kissed his chest, sliding her hands lower over the flat, ridged muscle of his belly. As her fingers closed over the silky hardness of his erection he let out a low groan and rolled her under him in one smooth motion.

Teeth clenched, he looked down at her, the driven need in his face sending a fresh wave of lustful longing through her. 'It has to be now, *cara*.'

Face hot, flushed, she nodded and closed her eyes, letting them half open as she heard him reach for a condom and sheathe himself. Then she felt the heat of him against the curls at the apex of her legs and took one deep breath, relaxing in a long, sibilant sigh as he slid into her, increasing the pressure as her body rhythmically tightened around him.

Her legs lifted, locking around his waist as every thrust took her deeper into the warm darkness, deeper into herself. She was more aware of herself than she ever had been, while also conscious of all of him, not just the place inside her he was touching. But him, the hardness of him, the heat... Danilo! Until the two became indistinguishable, where he began and where she ended unimportant, and they arrived at the same place at the same moment; their cries became one.

Tess floated back from the place he had taken her and opened her eyes to find Danilo watching her.

He gave a wolfish grin, still stunned by their primal coupling made more amazing because she came to him a virgin. 'Are you all right? I didn't mean—'

'I found it pretty wonderful. I'm left wondering if all egomaniacs are equally good lovers.' She missed his answering frown. She was asleep.

CHAPTER TEN

'HAD A GOOD NIGHT?'

Natalia smiled. 'Perfect. The best birthday ever,' she said, stifling a yawn and adding a rueful, 'Sorry!'

'You're exhausted.'

'A bit tired, but I'm fine.'

'You're not fine, you should go to bed—'

'I can't. I have to thank people and say goodbye and—'

Danilo pressed a light kiss to her forehead. 'All things I think I can do on your behalf. You go to bed.'

'Well, if you're sure?'

'I am,' he said firmly. 'Consider it part of your birthday present.'

'Danilo, Tess looks lovely tonight, doesn't she?'

He tensed, and silently amended, Tess looked *spectacular*. 'Where is this leading?'

'She's been here five weeks, she's due to leave next week.'

Five weeks and the last couple had been spent in his bed. That fire showed no signs of burning itself out. He was beginning to wonder if there was a way for her to stay longer. 'Yes, I know.'

'Can't you say something that will make her stay? I just hate the idea of her not being here.'

His jaw clenched. 'What do you want me to do, kidnap her?'

He saw her expression and moderated his tone, adding lightly, 'Maybe you could visit her there? Take a trip to London?'

'It won't be the same.' Natalia sighed.

An hour later Danilo had performed the last of the formal farewells, a situation that had paid surprising dividends when a handshake from one of the last VIP guests to leave had closed a deal that he had not expected to be finalised for weeks yet, so the evening had been a triumph on more than one level.

Danilo was now standing on the empty helipad when the head of the security detail approached him. He arched a brow. 'Problem?'

The ex-army, suited figure shook his head.

'Nothing of note. Just to let you know we'll do one final sweep of the grounds and then wind things down.'

Danilo glanced towards the thin ribbon of silver light created by the last of the cars as they moved down the drive and nodded. 'Good job.' He loosened his tie as the man walked away, speaking into his earpiece, before setting off in the opposite direction. He had his own plans to wind down too.

Fuelled by urgency, Danilo strode back towards the *palazzo*, crossing the terrace, which earlier had been packed with people but was empty now, save for the catering staff who were piling empty glasses and discarded champagne bottles onto trays with quiet efficiency.

Conscious of a steady buzz of anticipation in his blood, Danilo entered the ballroom where the band were packing up their instruments. He paused, his eyes moving around the room, searching as he had been doing all night, only now he did not need to be covert about it. It was not a guilty pleasure—just a pleasure.

He no longer had to fight the tug. He *could* cross the room, he *could* breathe in her fragrance. Obviously he could not have spent the evening with her beside him, an indulgence that would have been misinterpreted or even been considered a public declaration of sorts; it would be unfair to expose her to that sort of speculation.

The knowledge had not lessened his sense of frustration as the evening had progressed and he had seen Tess dancing with other men, smiling at other men, laughing up at other men.

Which was good! He had *wanted* her to enjoy herself, not hide in a corner. Not that such a thing would have been possible in that eye-wateringly sexy green dress, but maybe he'd wanted her not to enjoy herself *that* much.

Dio, who was he kidding? He hadn't wanted her to enjoy herself at all without him, he had wanted her. Just wanted her, beside him, with him…for them to be an official couple—and it was not possible.

Why not?

The question, so unexpected that he had no set answer to fall back on, sent a vibration of shock through Danilo. He had put his personal life on hold after the accident to focus on Natalia. It had been a choice and perhaps there had, he realised, been an element of the hair shirt about it, a way to expiate his sins; he *deserved* to suffer, not that he would ever suffer as much as his sister had.

Even then, he thought contemptuously, his sacrifice had not gone as far as abstinence. He had justified this by thinking of these disposable liaisons as a practical release valve that left him with nothing but an empty feeling. Had any of this not so *noble sacrifice* helped Natalia?

The only thing it had proved was that he was a shallow, selfish bastard.

When he had begun sleeping with Tess it had been meant to be more of the same, but she was a very different sort of woman. He had always known that, but it had felt safe because she would be out of his life very soon. She would be out of his life. His lips compressed, self-disgust a metallic taste in his mouth.

With a painful and uncomfortable flash of insight he suddenly saw tonight from her point of view. He had acted as though he were ashamed of her, that she wasn't good enough for his friends, whereas in reality she was too good for them, and too good for him.

The tightness in his chest increased as he stared at the woman he had fallen into a relationship with. The question was, had he fallen in love with her too?

Suddenly he saw the evening as fighting his instincts to prove to himself that he could, to prove to himself that nothing had happened, as something very different. But if he felt that putting her at a distance would have prevented the truth that was hammering away inside his skull he could not have been more wrong.

A young man carrying a tray neatly side-stepped to avoid a collision when Danilo stopped dead without warning. He stood there amid the detritus of the festivities, staring at the figure who stood beside the piano player, the internal conflict stamped on his lean features.

The pianist, a young man who'd had a crowd of admirers around him all night, a fact Danilo suspected was attributable as much to his blue eyes as his talent, was smiling up at her, laughing while his fingers moved casually across the keys.

This time Danilo did not fight any impulses. He crossed the room in seconds and slid his arm across her shoulders, pulling her into his side.

'I've been looking for you.'

'I've been right here.' She lowered her chin

to hide the hurt she knew he would see in her eyes, then, turning her head into his chest, she let herself stay there, giving herself a moment before she tilted her head back to meet his eyes. 'Has everyone gone?'

Of course they had, or he wouldn't be here now talking to her, after ignoring her all evening. She pushed away the quiver of resentment.

You knew what you were getting into, Tess, so no point crying foul now. He had never pretended. Sometimes she wished he would, which probably made her weak, or an idiot, or both?

If she'd been asked to put their relationship into words it would have sounded furtive... even sordid and, yes, there were moments when she asked herself what she was doing. Asked herself what had happened to her pride. But those moments never outlasted his kiss. When they were together everything felt *right*.

But tonight, as she had watched him from a distance as he'd worked the room, as important and powerful people had vied for his attention, she'd realised that she had started to live for those moments when the door closed and the rest of the world went away.

The fear the knowledge brought with it went

soul deep. She had always prided herself on facing the truth but tonight had made her realise how close she had come to reading more into his desire than was there, of convincing herself that their love-making could not be so perfect if there was no emotional connection underlying it. She had forgotten that simply wanting something to be didn't make it happen.

For Danilo what they shared was sex, great sex, but just sex. This was the reality; tonight was the reality. In bed they were lovers and outside she was nothing to him and next week she would be less than nothing, a memory.

'Not quite everyone, *cara*. We are here.' He half turned her as his warm hands slid down her shoulders, pulling her into him. 'And I have just realised that we have not had a dance.' He glanced towards the young pianist, who nodded, and a moment later the room was filled with the sad, sweet sound of a classic romantic ballad.

Danilo tipped his head, the formality of the gesture in sharp contrast to the sensual glow in his eyes, which stayed on her face. 'May I?'

Tess hesitated and pulled away a little.

Danilo frowned. 'Is something wrong?'

She could have said, *Yes, I've fallen in love*

with you and I have no pride left. But she didn't. Tomorrow was soon enough…one last night and then tomorrow she'd walk through the door before it was closed in her face, salvaging at least a little pride.

Her throat thick with emotion, Tess shook her head.

The furrow between his dark brows relaxed as, holding her gaze, he took her hands and placed them on his shoulders. After covering one with his own he placed his free hand in the small of her back before beginning to move to the music.

'I can't dance,' she cautioned, struggling to hide the deep sadness inside her. 'I'll tread on your toes.'

'A price worth paying to hold you close, *cara*,' he whispered in her ear.

The combination of the husky sentiment and the waft of his warm breath on her ear made Tess shiver. Eyes closed, she leaned her face against his chest, aware of the strong, heavy thud of his heartbeat. A couple of bars in and she had forgotten about her two left feet. It was that rare thing—a *perfect* moment. Everything else vanished and there was only the man who held her and the music and them together as one.

The people still working in the room stopped what they were doing to watch the duo who circled the room and others, drawn by the sound of the virtuoso performance by the young man who was destined one day to headline at opera houses all over the world, appeared at doorways and stood watching as the couple circling the floor, oblivious to the audience and their surroundings, lost in the music and each other, continued to move as one.

'The music has stopped, Danilo.' It was still in her head. She would never forget the sound—they had a song but no relationship... how ironic was that?

'I know.'

'People are staring.'

'Let them.' They were still moving to the music playing in her head—could he hear it too? The silk of Tess's dress hissed against the marble floor as Danilo twirled her out through the doors and onto the terrace before finally stopping. It was totally deserted now; the extra tables had gone and the moonlit night was silent.

Danilo hooked a finger under her chin and forced her face up to his. As their eyes meshed he took a deep breath, struggling to identify the unfamiliar feeling that tightened his gut as nervousness.

'I have to check on Nat. She had a headache. Then…'

One last night, she added silently, *to remember.*

The emotional ache in her throat threatening to emerge as tears, Tess blinked hard to stop them spilling and raised herself on tiptoe. The glow in his eyes as their glances connected—she could have easily read more into it than simple lust but she wouldn't let herself—made her head spin.

'I'll be waiting,' she said simply before she brushed her lips lightly over his.

The tantalising contact drew a groan from his throat. He hooked a hand behind her head and kissed her back with a hunger that made her knees sag. She clung to him for a moment after he pulled back.

'Don't be too long.'

Desire flared hotly in his eyes at the plea. 'I won't be.' Urgency made his voice raw as his soul-stripping scrutiny slid over the curves of her body, outlined in clinging green silk. 'Don't take it off. I want to.'

He was in the lift that gave direct access to his sister's suite when his phone rang. A glance at the number drew his brow into a frown.

'I'm sorry, I've just realised what time it is… I'll ring back tomorrow.'

Danilo cut across the British consultant's apology. 'Now is fine.'

'I know your sister cancelled her last appointment but I just wanted to be sure—does she want to reschedule?'

The lift drew to a smooth halt but Danilo did not move. 'My sister cancelled her appointment?'

'I assumed…' The other man's discomfort was obvious in his voice as he added quickly, 'No matter. I will discuss it with her tomorrow. It's just her phone was off. Don't worry, I'll speak with her tomorrow.'

Danilo slid the phone back into his pocket and stood there staring at the blank wall. Natalia had cancelled an appointment? He did not know that she had even had an appointment, and now she had cancelled?

He flinched as guilt hit him in the gut with the force of a sledgehammer blow. This was what happened when he took his eye off the ball, when he forgot where his priorities, his duty lay. This had happened because for the past couple of weeks he had spent his days thinking about nights with Tess.

Why was he even asking himself if he loved her? The question was irrelevant. He couldn't afford to be in love. Besides, Tess deserved a man who could give her more than he was able to offer.

He straightened his shoulders, prepared for what was to come, but as the doors slid silently open he realised that actually he wasn't!

Despite the promise Danilo made, the ice in the bucket that held the unopened bottle of champagne Tess had carried up to her room had dissolved into water by the time her bedroom door finally opened.

Normally Danilo slipped quietly into her room. This time there was nothing furtive about his appearance, but Tess, who was sitting on the bed at the time, did not make the mistake of reading anything good into the fact, as he'd wrenched the door open so hard the solid oak had rattled on its hinges.

When he slammed it behind him with equal force and turned his cold, contemptuous stare on her face the moment stretched and her dismayed confusion increased.

She'd seen Danilo frustrated and snappy,

she had seen him irritated, she thought she'd seen him angry. Now she realised that she was wrong. She hadn't.

The Danilo standing there, his body clenched, every sinew taut, the golden skin blanched of colour as it stretched tight across his razor-sharp cheekbones that were scored with dull dark colour—now, *this* was angry. This was *furious*!

And all that fury was aimed at her, Tess realised, struggling to think past the shocked bemusement in her befuddled brain.

His taut body was literally quivering with outrage. Standing there, he managed to look simultaneously magnificent and scary, but most of all *furious*!

She pressed her lips together, tasting the strawberry gloss she had coated them with several times while she'd waited, trying to work out what was happening and more importantly why.

In contrast to his actions and rigid stance, Danilo's voice was lethally soft when he finally spoke. 'So, what are we celebrating?'

She watched as, without another word, he walked across to the ice bucket, pulled out the bottle and, with a sharp twist, popped the cork. The champagne exploded in a fountain, leaving barely enough to cover the bottom of the two glasses. He picked up one and raised it.

'A toast. To lies and liars everywhere, and especially to those we know and love.'

Tess ignored the glass. Her head was spinning in confusion. The anxiety in her stomach was making her feel sick. 'What has happened?'

'Oh, you know—same old, same old. Oh, and I have just walked in on my sister with her boyfriend, my sister who has cancelled her appointment with the consultant.'

'Oh, no!' Tess closed her eyes and when she opened them again sympathy glowed in them. 'I'm so sorry, Danilo.'

His jaw clenched as he fought to regain some level of control. He had been a fool but he would not fall for her soft sympathy again. 'And this comes as such a shock to you?' he drawled. 'Any of it?'

'No,' she admitted. 'I knew that she'd been seeing Marco. She cares for him, Danilo, and I really think that he cares for her. Where is the harm? She's a grown woman, Danilo. She has to make her own mistakes.'

'Easy enough for someone who isn't going to be around to pick up the pieces after those mistakes to say,' he sneered, refusing to acknowledge the hurt in her eyes. 'You wreak damage like some blasted tsunami.'

Her chin came up. 'It's not my fault and I'm sick and tired of you blaming me when anything goes wrong!'

Her protest was drowned out by the sound of the glass he was holding splintering in his hand.

'Danilo! You're bleeding! Let me...'

He looked at the blood dripping from his hand without interest and snapped, 'Leave it!'

She gave a shrug. 'Fine. Bleed to death!' she tossed back childishly. 'What exactly is wrong with your sister having a boyfriend? And don't try and tell me this is about Marco. You'd be the same about any man she dated. Has it even crossed your mind that Marco's feelings are genuine?'

'She is in a wheelchair.'

Her patience snapped—talk about tunnel vision! 'Well, maybe Marco can see beyond the wheelchair. Unlike you!' She watched him pale with anger at the accusation and her own anger drained away. 'You're not protecting her, Danilo,' she said softly. 'You're—' She stopped, shaking her head.

'I'm what?'

'You're smothering her.' There was no accusation in the words, just deep sadness.

'I will get her out of the wheelchair—' And yet he hadn't. All his life he had achieved whatever he set out to and now the only thing he wanted to do was eluding him.

'And what if you can't?' she countered quietly. 'What if—?'

'How long have you been filling Natalia's head with this sort of defeatist attitude?'

'Nat is the least defeatist person I have ever met. She is brave and strong and upbeat. I haven't brainwashed Nat. I couldn't. She is as stubborn and pig-headed as you are.'

'How long have you known?'

'Does it matter?' she asked wearily.

'Did you think it was amusing to plot behind my back?'

Her eyes blinked wide at the accusation. 'There was no plotting, there was no—'

'And you knew my feelings on the subject.' The sweep of his cold eyes made her shiver.

'I found out by accident and what was I meant to do? She—' Aware that her explanation could seem as if she wasn't taking responsibility for her actions, she bit her lip and, shaking her head, lowered her chin to her chest.

'You were meant,' he ground out, 'to tell me. It's my job to protect her. She is vulnerable, an easy target. It's my fault she is in that chair, the least I can do is—'

As he broke off, swearing, Tess's chin came up. 'How is it your fault? It was a car accident. Weren't you in another country at the time?'

'I was in bed at the time.'

'Not yours?' she said, knowing the answer even before she read his expression.

He half turned, presenting his classical profile to her. Even at this distance she could see the tense quiver of fine muscles beneath his golden-toned skin. 'I was meant to join my family for a birthday celebration, but I had a better offer.'

The hollow sound of his laugh made her wince.

'If I had been there that night I would have been at the wheel and who knows? My reflexes are forty years younger than my father's were, but we never will know.' He dragged a hand across his dark hair and turned back to her. 'Because I put sex with a woman whose name I can't remember ahead of a promise. I will not do that again.' And yet he almost had; his innate selfishness had reasserted itself again. 'I made a promise to Natalia that she would walk again and nothing or…no one will get in the way of that.' Certainly not an affair with a woman he could not trust. Well, at least, he thought heavily, he had found out in time before he made a total fool of himself.

Well, at least she knew now and nothing she could have done or not done would have altered the situation. Tess unfolded her legs from under her and slid off the bed where she had sat frozen since he had walked in. The swishing sound of the green silk on the floor sounded loud as she walked barefoot towards him.

Avoiding her eyes, his glance was snagged and caught by the thin spaghetti strap that had slid down one smooth shoulder.

'So this is really all about you and your guilt, your redemption, and not about Nat at all. You were not responsible for the accident because it was just that. If you'd been there that night you might be the one in a wheel-chair.' Her eyes darkened. 'Or worse.'

'There is no worse,' he countered grimly.

Suddenly she felt very angry.

'How long will it take you to forget my name, Danilo?' She had gone beyond anger;

there was just intense sadness in her soft voice.

'It was only ever sex. What the hell are you doing?'

Tess lifted her chin. 'Liar!' she charged. 'And I'm packing. I'm leaving because I'm sick of taking the blame for everything bad that happens in your life. I'm sick of it always being about *your* feelings, *your* needs. I'm sick of being our dirty secret because I thought the sex is good, but, you know, it's not that good!' she finished on a breathless note of antagonism.

The anger and fight suddenly drained out of her.

'Do you even think you've done anything wrong?' Without pause for her response, Danilo continued his ruthless and unfair analysis of the situation, answering his own question in a voice that was harsh with condemnation. 'Of course you did. You're not stupid, and I think that you didn't just *know*, I think you lent your assistance to the affair. You know Nat's vulnerable, but that didn't matter to you, did it? You are so damned convinced that you know what is best…you just can't resist meddling…'

Hands clenched, he leaned his head against

the wall and, chest heaving, took several deep breaths as he pressed his fingers against his temples where anger pulsed and pounded.

'I think that without you there would not have been an affair.'

'It had been going on long before I arrived.'

He brushed aside the irrelevant detail with a wave of his hand. 'You knew that I wanted to keep that boy away from Nat.'

'Like I said, Danilo, it's not always about what *you* want.' She slammed the lid closed on the case with a bang.

'You planning on travelling like that?'

Without a word she stepped out of her dress.

Danilo swore and swung away. The hell of it was he *wanted*...he just *wanted*. Arms folded across his chest, he continued to stare out of the window.

'Does anyone live up to your standards, Danilo?' she wondered.

Nostrils flared, he turned back, Tess was standing there zipping up her jeans. She gave a loud sniff. Acknowledging that part of him still couldn't hear that sniff without wanting to comfort her only intensified the levels of his outrage.

'Well, you sure as hell don't!'

'You really are an obnoxious son of a…' She picked up her case and stalked to the door and he didn't make a move to stop her.

CHAPTER ELEVEN

WHEN TESS ARRIVED back in London she got in a taxi and went straight to her flat. For the first time in her life the take-off and landing had not bothered her. The entire flight was a blur. She had felt numb and strangely disconnected from what was happening around her as she sat in the back of the taxi listening to the driver chat.

She felt as though she had been holding her breath since she had walked out of her bedroom, and it wasn't until she closed the door of her flat behind her that she gave herself permission to breathe.

And feel. It was like walking into a wall of pain: unbearable!

With a cry she fell to her knees and, forehead pressed to the ground, began to weep. Keening sobs that seemed dragged from a place deep inside her.

She had no idea how long the storm lasted but when it was over she didn't have the strength to get up so she lay where she was and fell asleep. It was the middle of the night when she woke up. She got to her feet, stepped over her case, which still lay where she had dropped it, and walked into the bedroom. Not pausing to remove her clothes, she flung herself on the bed and slept again.

That set the pattern for the next forty-eight hours: sleep punctuated by crying bouts. On the third day she looked at her dull-eyed reflection in the mirror and felt a wave of self-disgust.

What the hell am I doing? she asked herself. *Other than acting like a total and complete gutless wonder?*

She took a deep breath and literally and mentally squared her shoulders. At twenty-six, most people she knew had loved and lost at least once. It wasn't as if what she was feeling was unique—no, that was Danilo. Teeth clenched, she pushed away the image of his face but not before the ache inside her had intensified to the point where she rocked her body to ease it.

Did the feeling ever go away? she wondered, feeling a retrospective stab of admiration for the people who had their hearts broken and didn't fall apart.

It wasn't even as if she had started out thinking there was any future between them. From Danilo's side it had never been anything more than a sort of holiday romance, without much romance. The place that had existed was in her head.

She had known it would end, she had prepared herself for it, she just hadn't expected the end to be so acrimonious.

She could take Danilo not loving her back but the idea of him out there somewhere hating her was almost unbearable. She lifted her chin and exhaled, pushing her hair behind her ears as she struggled to push past that pain. She *would* bear it because she hadn't been raised to feel sorry for herself; she hadn't been raised to quit.

She showered and realised she hadn't eaten for days and checked out her store cupboard. A can of soup was about the only instant food she could find, so after she had eaten it she went out to shop. All so normal but so not normal.

Tess began to wonder if actually *anything* would ever be the same again. Would she be stuck in this cycle for ever? Her mood swinging wildly between deep despair, self-pity and anger?

That night she woke up at two in the morning wanting Danilo's touch so much that the pain made her think she was having a heart attack.

When it had passed, she lay there thinking, *If this is love, they can keep it.*

She'd been home a week before she felt able to ring Fiona without falling apart. She gave her friend an expurgated version of the summer's events and half an hour later Fiona landed on the doorstep with a bottle of wine in one hand, a carrier bag of chocolate bars in the other.

'Let's get drunk and fat.'

Tess appreciated the thought but the smell of the wine made her feel nauseous, so she passed. Not that it lessened the enjoyment of the evening, which came from being able to step away from her sadness for at least a few hours. It gave her some hope that one day she would be able to step away from it permanently, that she wasn't doomed to walk around feeling as though she had a large weight attached to her chest for ever.

She rang her mum the next day, expecting a lecture on self-reliance and toughness. Only to be surprised when her parent reacted with sympathy, and when Tess admitted she had spent the last week wallowing, instead of her mum telling her to man up she shocked Tess by saying, 'It was probably the best thing but maybe it's time to move on now?'

Later, she turned up at Tess's door, though her therapy was slightly different—a stack of election leaflets. She made Tess laugh when she suggested that pushing them through doors might be therapeutic.

Actually she was right—it was...weirdly.

Tess was glad when the first day of term finally arrived—the days that preceded it had felt like a lifetime—but as she stepped into the classroom and saw all the fresh, eager faces it felt like a clean-slate start.

She was going to look forwards, not sit in a corner and cry for what she'd lost because the things she was weeping for were things she'd never really had. She was lucky, she told herself, to be doing something she loved. Something that was fulfilling and challenging.

The start of a new school year was always hectic and this year particularly so. At the end of the first week Tess was feeling tired and drained, but she didn't read anything into it, not until the following Monday when, before the lunch bell rang, she felt so faint and dizzy that she had to sit down with her head between her knees to wait for it to pass. While she sat there, her classroom assistant, Lily had called an ambulance.

Luckily, she recovered enough to cancel the ambulance that was being dispatched, but it was still a very embarrassing incident. Even though it seemed a waste of time to her, she agreed when the deputy head made her promise to make an appointment to see her doctor.

Quite willing and fully expecting to wait for an appointment—she could not be classed as an emergency—Tess was surprised when they said they had a cancellation if she could come right away. The deputy head, who was standing there listening in, commandeered the phone and spoke. 'Yes, she can.'

'But I feel fine now.'

Tess said the same thing when she explained what had happened to the doctor.

She walked out of the surgery half an hour later not feeling fine at all. Her legs felt like cotton wool, her knees were shaking and her brain had shut down.

It wasn't until she found herself standing, looking in a shop window just around the corner from her flat, repeating what she had said to the doctor out loud—*But I feel fine*—that she realised two things. She probably wasn't fine and she had left her car in the surgery car park.

She decided to leave her car until the morning and walk the rest of the way home. She was so dazed that she didn't immediately see the person waiting outside her building for her until her name had been called out twice.

Her initial thought was, *So I'm not pregnant, just mad.*

'Tess, are you all right?'

Tess blinked. *Am* I *all right?* Natalia Raphael was sitting ten feet away, a suitcase on her knee and a wary look on her face.

'Nat, what are you doing here?'

Natalia gave a loud sniff. 'I have left home.' She then began to sob in earnest. 'Since you left Danilo has been totally impossible and when I said that if he wouldn't let me see Marco I would leave, he did that looking-down-his-nose thing…you know what I mean.'

Tess felt a pang of envy; she did.

'And I told him that Marco graduated top of his class, even though he was working two jobs, and he was the best thing that ever happened to me and you know what he did then?'

'Before or after he stopped swearing?'

'He didn't even do that so obviously I left. I said I would.'

In other words Danilo had pushed her into a corner. Oh, but he was going to be frantic!

'So Danilo doesn't know where you are?'

'No and you can't tell him ever. Can I stay with you?'

'I thought you'd want to be with Marco?'

'Marco is as bad as Danilo. He said that I was being impulsive and I should go talk with my brother. *Talk*—I ask you!'

'Oh, dear.'

'Can I?'

'I'd love to have you stay with me but...' she glanced over her shoulder '...my flat is on the top floor and there isn't a lift.' She took a deep breath. 'But don't worry—I have an idea.'

Her mum arrived at the café when she and Nat were on their second cup of coffee, or at least Nat was. Tess had felt queasy after the first sip and spent the rest of the time stirring it.

Tess made the introductions. She had already given her mum the bare bones of the situation on the phone. 'Mum has a ground-floor flat and she has plenty of room.' She left the two to chat while she excused herself.

Tess hissed in frustration as she struggled

to get a signal on her phone from the ladies' room, and when she finally managed to get through to Danilo's mobile number it went straight to the messaging service.

She really couldn't bear the thought of his frantic reaction when he discovered his sister missing. Tess backed up her voice message with a text, just in case.

Danilo might hate her, but if she had learnt anything over the past few hellish weeks it was that, regardless of what he thought of her, she would always love him. She would never have him but she would have his baby. She glanced down, a wondering smile flickering across her mouth as she pressed a hand to her stomach as the reality finally penetrated the blank fog of panic and denial that had been her initial reaction.

She felt oddly calm, which was not rational. Her life was about to change and there was the task of telling Danilo. She had literally no idea what his reaction would be.

She wasn't even sure she would see him when he came for his sister—she had included her mum's number in the message—but if she did was now the right time to tell him? Or should she get used to the idea herself first?

Was there ever a right time?

Pushing the question away, she went back into the café, stifling a stab of guilt when she saw Nat deep in conversation with her mum.

She doubted it would matter to Natalia that Tess had not actually made any promises, but even if she had Tess had no intention of repeating her mistake. Not that doing the right thing on this occasion would mitigate what she had done in Danilo's eyes previously, but just as Tess felt she had acted in Nat's best interests last time, she felt she was doing so this time too—but then *right*, she thought sadly, was very much a subjective thing.

'Did you know that your mum knows Dame Eva Black?' Natalia said the name of the famous visually impaired athlete with awe.

'Name-dropping again, Mum?'

'Don't be rude, and ungrateful. Eva sent you those tickets for your school auction.'

'That's great. Please thank my godmother for me.'

'Godmother? Wow!'

'Right, we are sorted. Nat and I are getting a taxi back to my place. Give her time to settle in and then you can join us for supper.' Beth leaned in a little closer and, under cover of kissing her daughter's cheek, whispered, 'Have you contacted her brother?'

Tess gave an imperceptible nod and her mother mouthed *good* before turning back to her house guest.

Once she'd seen them safely into a cab, Tess walked the short distance to her flat where for the second time that day she found a Raphael waiting for her on her doorstep.

Her heart stopped beating for a second and then compensated by climbing into her throat, beating so hard she could barely breathe.

He looked so familiar. Tall, sleek, unbelievably elegant and yet there were differences too. He was thinner, the body fat had burned off him—not that he had ever carried much—making him look harder and more...*hungry*. It showed in his face, the skin stretched tighter emphasising the angle and prominence of his cheekbones. She stood there absorbing the details with the hunger of an addict deprived of her drug of choice for too long.

He read the note that Marco had brought him for the second time and laughed.

There was a dark irony to it. He had told himself that he was doing the right thing, the noble thing. He had put his life on hold for his sister. He had walked away from love, and did she appreciate this *noble* sacrifice? No! She wrote a note, in which he was labelled as a control freak, and ran away.

He inhaled, closing his eyes as he screwed up the paper in his hand. The situation forced his hand…he'd wanted everything to be perfect, but then life was not perfect.

Noble. Who was he kidding? Not himself any longer at any rate. He wasn't taking the noble route, he was taking the easy route. Pride had stopped him calling her back and cowardice had made him push her away.

Tess had been right when she'd accused him of using her as a scapegoat, whereas in reality she had brought only good into their lives. Deep inside he'd always known that; he had struggled not to love her because he didn't think he deserved to be happy while Nat sat in a wheelchair. Tess had said it was always about him and she was right… Had he ever once asked her what she wanted?

It was time he did.

He levered himself off the wall, the speech he had practised on the flight vanishing when he saw her. 'Hello, *cara mia.*'

Was he trying to be deliberately cruel?

Before he could say anything she rushed headlong into an explanatory speech. 'She is safe with my mum. I tried to contact you. I left messages. This was not my doing, and I didn't put her up to this, Danilo, and I'm not in the mood for one of your rants so please just go away!'

'I never thought you did...' But he had known where Nat would run. 'With *your mother*?'

She nodded, not quite sure what to make of this Danilo, who wasn't shouting or flinging accusations. The stillness about him confused her. 'The stairs.'

'Of course. I remember.' He remembered everything.

'How,' she puzzled, 'are you here now?'

'She left Marco a note, and to his credit he brought it to me as soon as he found it. He... We were pretty sure if she was going to run it would be to you.'

It was a compulsion that he understood well.

'It seems that I might—' He broke off, his heart contracting painfully as he took in the dark shadows smudged beneath her spectacular eyes. Her skin was so pale it seemed almost transparent. He fought down the urge to run his fingers over it, knowing it would be smooth and satiny to the touch. She looked fragile, breakable; he struggled past the need to wrap her in his arms.

'Might?' she prompted.

'I might have misjudged him. But everyone deserves a second chance, don't you think?'

The intensity of his stare made her nervous. His being here at all made her nervous! Thinking about how to tell him, when to tell him… the words, the tone to take…made her nervous. 'I…yes, I suppose. You must be anxious to see Nat. I can give you the address. I have a piece of paper here somewhere.' She began to search the deep pockets of the light belted trench coat she was wearing over her skirt and blouse.

'She is safe?'

Tess nodded. 'She might be wielding a protest banner when you see her next but she is fine.'

'Then no, I am not anxious to see her.'

She searched his face, seeking a clue that would explain the way he was behaving. 'You're not angry with her, are you?' Her jaw set. 'Because if you plan to yell at her the way—'

'No, I am not angry with *her.*' Only himself for being an utter imbecile. He had had paradise within his grasp and he'd walked in the opposite direction.

She heard the emphasis and thought, *So he's angry with* me. Pulling her hands from her pockets, she crossed them in front of her in an unconsciously self-protective gesture. No change there, then!

'Oh, hell, does it even matter?'

'Does what even matter?'

What's the point? It doesn't matter how you say it, or when, he's going to be furious.

'Danilo, I'm pregnant.'

His reaction to the blunt pronouncement was slow but when the look of shock appeared it was total. 'Pregnant?'

Her chin lifted to a challenging angle. 'Yes, and before you ask it's yours.'

'I never thought otherwise.'

'I suppose there hasn't been much time for it to be anyone else's.'

'Were you looking?' he growled out, the image of Tess falling into bed with another man seriously testing his determination to let her see that he was a changed man capable of calm control, the sort of man she deserved.

His comment released a fresh burst of anger inside her as the many, many *low* lights of the past few hellish weeks passed before her eyes. 'Sure, Danilo, it's been party, party all the way, what between throwing up and fainting in work. What the *hell* do you think I've been doing for the last few weeks, Danilo?' she demanded, as, hands on hips, she advanced until she was standing a foot away from him. 'Well?' she charged in a furious growl.

'I appreciate that it must have been hard for you, discovering you're pregnant...'

'I didn't even know I was until a few hours ago and that is the one *good* thing that has happened to me.'

'Good?' Freed from the self-imposed restraints—the effort of containing his delight and noisily expressing it had been a strain—he released a long sigh. He no longer had to hide his feelings in an effort to be sensitive to the anger and bitterness she might have been feeling, had every right to be feeling. An unplanned pregnancy was not every woman's idea of good.

A baby. He closed his eyes and let the warmth flow through him.

He couldn't even look at her! Tess ignored the hurt and embraced her anger as she lifted her chin and stood there in an attitude of angry defiance. 'Yes, I am, and—'

When Danilo opened his eyes he could see how paper thin her attitude was. In a way it emphasised how fragile she was. 'I will look after you...both.'

'Look after? I don't want looking after,' she choked out while the voice inside her head screamed, *I don't want looking after, I want loving!*

Danilo did not let the rejection deter him. 'Nonetheless, it is going to happen.'

She lifted both hands to her head, grabbing a handful of hair. 'Do you ever listen to anyone? I don't need you!' The lie emerged as a plaintive wail of despair.

'Fine, but I need you and, as you know, I am a selfish man.'

She stopped, the tears she struggled to blink away trembling on her eyelashes as she stared up at him, suspicion warring with hope in her face. 'You need me?'

He tipped his head. 'Yes, in a need oxygen, need water sort of way. You are one of the essentials to life for me.' He spoke with the total certainty of someone who had imagined a life without Tess in it and knew that breathing was not the same as being alive.

The journey to self-awareness had been slow and painful, speeded by the truths jolted free when he'd discovered Nat's disappearance, but before he had reached this point it had taken Danilo a week of raging against the fate that had brought Tess into his life, alternating between anger and self-pity while he congratulated himself on being rid of her.

He hadn't asked to fall in love, he'd *wanted* to be punished, so when it had happened to him he had rejected it. He had rejected her and at the first excuse that had come he had pushed her away. But not the feelings she had awoken in him; they, he realised, would stay for ever. Love was as permanent as his fingerprints.

He had had everything a man could want and he had turned his back on it. Yes, he was an idiot and a coward!

His first instinct had been to get on a plane, but at the last moment he had paused. Tess had given him everything and in return... Self-disgust churned in his belly when he thought of the way he had treated her. He had never given her a word of tenderness, no romance, but he would!

He'd planned the proposal down to the smallest detail. The restaurant was booked, the singer he knew was her favourite was performing just for them and the chef he'd shipped in from New York. The only thing he was waiting for was the ring, which was still in the jeweller's—the one he had finally settled on had been far too big for her tiny fingers.

He had thought of everything except the unexpected, so here he was no ring, no romantic music, not even a straggly bunch of flowers… and definitely no script. That had gone out of the window the moment she had made her stunning revelation.

'What did you say?'

He couldn't think of any prettier way to say it so he just said what was in his heart. 'I love you.'

She tried to react with her head to the declaration, but she struggled to tune out the contribution of her hopeful heart, which was thudding like a wild thing in her chest. 'Is this about the baby?'

'I suppose everything from now on will be about the baby, but, no, irrespective of a baby or ten babies, I love you. I have loved you, and I would have been there to ask you—look, this isn't the way I planned it but, please, will you marry me, Tess? I don't know if you can ever forgive me for being such a total fool, because I am, but I'm a fool that loves you and I can change—'

'Oh, Danilo!' The cry came directly from her heart as she hit him like a heat-seeking missile, forcing the breath out of his lungs in a soft hiss.

'So does this mean you do forgive me?'

'I'll be your lover, your mistress, your wife. I'll be anything if I can be with you and I don't want you to change. I fell in love with you the way you are.'

Danilo swallowed, emotion thickening his voice as he responded to her emotional declaration. 'You are the most all-or-nothing person I have ever met and I'll settle for all: lover, mistress and wife.'

Oblivious to the stares of several passersby and the honking of a few horns the couple kissed and carried on kissing until a remark from someone in a car brought Danilo's head up.

'Get a room,' he repeated. 'He has a point.'

'I have a room,' she pointed out. 'I can walk now,' she protested as he swept her up.

'Just let me pretend I'm boss, at least in public, *cara mia*, for the sake of my fragile male ego. In private I will be whatever you want.'

EPILOGUE

Three years later

EVERY EYE IN the place was on the bride, all except one pair. Danilo's eyes were trained on his wife's face. Tears were running down her cheeks as she stood there in the silliest hat he had ever seen, looking more beautiful than any woman who had ever breathed. That she loved him still filled him with wonder, pride was mingled with that wonder as his gaze slid down her body. Her outfit had not been designed to hide the swelling of her belly that made him so proud.

The baby due in three months had been planned this time. A little brother or sister for their son, who walked proudly, bearing the bride's train in his chubby hands, the determination not to trip over it as he had done in the rehearsal clear in his face.

He heard Tess release a relieved sigh as the bride reached the altar where the groom, Marco, who had finally accepted Danilo's offer to join their legal team after being persuaded nepotism had nothing to do with it, was standing.

'She made it,' Tess whispered, tears in her eyes.

'Of course she did,' Danilo said as he rested the crutches he had held just in case the bride, who had been determined to walk down the aisle unaided, had needed them.

It had been Nat's decision in the end to go through with the experimental surgery, two more had followed and the physical therapy that had followed would have tested the resilience of a hardened soldier, but Nat had come through. The day she took her first step had been the day the young couple had announced their engagement.

There wasn't a dry eye in the house as the bride made her responses in a clear, confident voice. There were tears in Tess's eyes when she turned to look at Danilo. He knew what she was thinking about because so was he: the moment that *they* had stood in that very spot and exchanged the same vows.

He had told her, later that night, that it had

been the first day of the rest of his life. His new life, he thought as her fingers tightened in understanding around his, was very, very good!

* * * * *

If you enjoyed this story, check out these other great reads from Kim Lawrence:

*ONE NIGHT TO WEDDING VOWS
HER NINE-MONTH CONFESSION
THE SINS OF SEBASTIAN REY-DEFOE
ONE NIGHT WITH MORELLI
THE HEARTBREAKER PRINCE
Available now!*

LARGER-PRINT BOOKS!
GET 2 FREE LARGER-PRINT NOVELS PLUS
2 FREE GIFTS!

HARLEQUIN®

Romance

From the Heart, For the Heart

LARGER-PRINT BOOKS!
GET 2 FREE LARGER-PRINT NOVELS PLUS
2 FREE GIFTS!

♦HARLEQUIN®

superromance®

More Story...More Romance

LARGER-PRINT BOOKS!
GET 2 FREE LARGER-PRINT NOVELS PLUS
2 FREE GIFTS!

◆ HARLEQUIN®

INTRIGUE
BREATHTAKING ROMANTIC SUSPENSE

YES! Please send me 2 FREE LARGER-PRINT Harlequin® Intrigue novels and my 2 FREE gifts (gifts are worth about $10). After receiving them, if I don't wish to receive any more books, I can return the shipping statement marked "cancel." If I don't cancel, I will receive 6 brand-new novels every month and be billed just $5.49 per book in the U.S. or $6.24 per book in Canada. That's a saving of at least 11% off the cover price! It's quite a bargain! Shipping and handling is just 50¢ per book in the U.S. and 75¢ per book in Canada.* I understand that accepting the 2 free books and gifts places me under no obligation to buy anything. I can always return a shipment and cancel at any time. Even if I never buy another book, the two free books and gifts are mine to keep forever.

199/399 HDN GHWN

Name	(PLEASE PRINT)

Address	Apt. #

City	State/Prov.	Zip/Postal Code

Signature (if under 18, a parent or guardian must sign)

Mail to the **Reader Service:**
IN U.S.A.: P.O. Box 1867, Buffalo, NY 14240-1867
IN CANADA: P.O. Box 609, Fort Erie, Ontario L2A 5X3

**Are you a subscriber to Harlequin® Intrigue books
and want to receive the larger-print edition?
Call 1-800-873-8635 today or visit www.ReaderService.com.**

* Terms and prices subject to change without notice. Prices do not include applicable taxes. Sales tax applicable in N.Y. Canadian residents will be charged applicable taxes. Offer not valid in Quebec. This offer is limited to one order per household. Not valid for current subscribers to Harlequin Intrigue Larger-Print books. All orders subject to credit approval. Credit or debit balances in a customer's account(s) may be offset by any other outstanding balance owed by or to the customer. Please allow 4 to 6 weeks for delivery. Offer available while quantities last.

Your Privacy—The Reader Service is committed to protecting your privacy. Our Privacy Policy is available online at www.ReaderService.com or upon request from the Reader Service.

We make a portion of our mailing list available to reputable third parties that offer products we believe may interest you. If you prefer that we not exchange your name with third parties, or if you wish to clarify or modify your communication preferences, please visit us at www.ReaderService.com/consumerchoice or write to us at Reader Service Preference Service, P.O. Box 9062, Buffalo, NY 14240-9062. Include your complete name and address.

HILP15

WESTERN (WP) PROMISES

YES! Please send me **The Western Promises Collection** in Larger Print. This collection begins with 3 FREE books and 2 FREE gifts (gifts valued at approx. $14.00 retail) in the first shipment, along with the other first 4 books from the collection! If I do not cancel, I will receive 8 monthly shipments until I have the entire 51-book Western Promises collection. I will receive 2 or 3 FREE books in each shipment and I will pay just $4.99 US/ $5.89 CDN for each of the other four books in each shipment, plus $2.99 for shipping and handling per shipment. *If I decide to keep the entire collection, I'll have paid for only 32 books, because 19 books are FREE! I understand that accepting the 3 free books and gifts places me under no obligation to buy anything. I can always return a shipment and cancel at any time. My free books and gifts are mine to keep no matter what I decide.

272 HCN 3070 472 HCN 3070

Name	(PLEASE PRINT)	
Address		Apt. #
City	State/Prov.	Zip/Postal Code

Signature (if under 18, a parent or guardian must sign)

Mail to the **Reader Service:**

IN U.S.A.: P.O. Box 1867, Buffalo, NY 14240-1867
IN CANADA: P.O. Box 609, Fort Erie, Ontario L2A 5X3

* Terms and prices subject to change without notice. Prices do not include applicable taxes. Sales tax applicable in N.Y. Canadian residents will be charged applicable taxes. This offer is limited to one order per household. All orders subject to approval. Credit or debit balances in a customer's account(s) may be offset by any other outstanding balance owed by or to the customer. Please allow 4 to 6 weeks for delivery. Offer available while quantities last. Offer not available to Quebec residents.

Your Privacy—The Reader Service is committed to protecting your privacy. Our Privacy Policy is available online at www.ReaderService.com or upon request from the Reader Service.

We make a portion of our mailing list available to reputable third parties that offer products we believe may interest you. If you prefer that we not exchange your name with third parties, or if you wish to clarify or modify your communication preferences, please visit us at www.ReaderService.com/consumerschoice or write to us at Reader Service Preference Service, P.O. Box 9062, Buffalo, NY 14240-9062. Include your complete name and address.